EMILY FRANCE

Rare Book Division, The New York Public Library. "Recopilacion Delas Cartas Qve Fveron embiadas de las Indias & Isles del Serenissimo rey d' Portugal, ..." *The New York Public Library Digital Collections.* 1557.

Published in the United States by Soho Teen
an imprint of
Soho Press, Inc.
853 Broadway
New York, NY 10003

Library of Congress Cataloging-in-Publication Data

France, Emily
Signs of you / Emily France.
1. Self-help groups—Fiction. 2. Grief—Fiction. 3. Relics—Fiction.
4. Supernatural—Fiction. 5. Future life—Fiction. 6. Love—Fiction. I. Title
PZ7.1.F73 Sig 2016 (print) I PZ7.1.F73 (ebook) [Fic]—dc23 2015048581

ISBN 978-1-61695-657-8
eISBN 978-1-61695-658-5

Interior design by Janine Agro, Soho Press, Inc.

Printed in the United States of America

10 9 8 7 6 5 4 3 2 1

For my husband, Kevin. A sparkling wit. The greatest gift.
And the best date to the ninth grade dance a girl could ask for.

I love you.

Chapter 1

Sighting

She's been dead two years when I see her in the grocery store. She's looking at bottles of bubble bath. She picks up a pink one, unscrews the cap, and sniffs. Her nose wrinkles and she puts the bottle back on the shelf. As she looks for a different scent, I blink.

I must be losing my mind. I look again. It's her.

Everything about her is how I remember it—her chestnut bobbed hair, her smooth golden skin and high cheekbones, her familiar blue sweater zipped up halfway. She's wearing the dress we buried her in, baby blue linen with a tiny floral print. I blink and blink again. It's her. I am looking at my mother. The mother I last saw in a coffin; the mother we buried at Richfield Cemetery two years ago last week. The mother who's dead because of me.

She picks up another bottle of bubble bath and reads the label. I take a step closer, and she looks up and smiles. When our eyes meet, I feel like I might collapse under the weight of everything I need to say. That I'm sorry for that night. That the last words I ever said to her were angry and mean and horrible. "I hate you," I'd said. *Hate, hate, hate.* And I'm sorry I didn't try to stop her as she ran out the door, upset and hurt, and got behind the wheel of a car we all knew she shouldn't have been driving. Not with her injury.

My mom wasn't supposed to drive because of me. When she gave birth to me, she got hurt. During labor, her blood pressure spiked and she had a stroke. It was a small one, but big enough to affect her sight and sometimes her memory. She always told me that she'd missed so much. She couldn't see well enough to teach me how to put on makeup, to ride a bike, to parallel park.

But when she said these things I knew she wasn't talking to me, or even about me. She'd been forced to give up driving, forced to quit the nursing job she'd loved. She'd missed out on a lot of the good stuff, on the dreamed-about, supposed-to-be stuff. All because I was born. And the last words I'd said to her, the mother whose life I'd ruined, were *I hate you.*

And as if screaming it wasn't enough, I ran to my room and tweeted it, too:

Hate my mom. Hate. #meanit.

I tweeted it because I didn't have that many followers. And I still don't. I've never been that popular online or anywhere else, really. But people found out about my tweet. It got retweeted. Then posted on Facebook. Quickly I became the girl who told her mom off the night she died. I vowed never to tweet another thing as long as I live, but that doesn't help. I'll never know how many people saw it; I can't pull it back and make it my own private shame. It's just . . . out there.

But now she's standing ten feet from me in the grocery store, and I have another chance. All I can think is *I'm sorry.* Sorry you had me, sorry I screwed up your life, sorry I said what I did. I want to hear her voice, to smell her perfume, to wrap my arms around the woman whose blood is my own. I want to say *Mom*. So I run. Well, I try to run. My feet won't work right. I put one foot in front of the other as fast as I can, but I'm dizzy and disoriented.

When I'm close, her beautiful smile changes to a look of horror. She shoves the bottle of bubble bath back on the shelf and walks away.

I speed up. So does she. She rounds the corner and I lose sight of her behind a huge display of crackers. I break into a sprint, clear the pyramid of boxes, and nearly bump into her.

She turns. Except now the woman who faces me looks nothing like my mother. She's a blonde, in hot pink lipstick. Her dress has lost its familiar floral print. Now, she's just wearing jeans.

"Can I help you?" the woman asks. My cheeks flush hot under the glare of the grocery store fluorescents.

"No, ma'am. I'm . . . I'm sorry. I thought you were someone else," I say.

The woman looks annoyed that I stopped her. Annoyed and maybe a little frightened. She shakes her head and hurries away. I watch her go and know that I *should* be thinking that I've lost my mind. But I'm not. At first, I'm thinking one thing, and one thing only:

Mom, come back.

But then another thought comes:

I think I know why I saw you.

I'M A MESS AS I pull out of Heinen's parking lot. My palms are sweaty; I can't get a good grip on the steering wheel. I feel frayed, my insides totally shattered, but instead of speeding,

I drive way too slowly. Like I'm afraid I'll hit something or someone at any moment because I can't focus on the road. A car comes up behind me and the driver lays on the horn. I look in my rearview mirror to see if I know the man behind the wheel, but all I catch is the blur of his SUV as he swerves around me and gives me the finger.

I start again, a little quicker this time, and catch sight of my hazel eyes in the rearview mirror. Maybe the guilt finally got to me. I *wanted* to stop Mom the night she ran out after our fight. As she brushed by me, car keys in hand, I wanted to shout. *Please, don't go*, the words were on the tip of my tongue. Chills ran down my arms like millions of tiny marbles under my skin. As I watched her slip out the door, some part of me *knew* she'd never come back through it. Or maybe that's just how I remember it. Maybe it's easier to convince myself that I knew I was going to lose her before I actually did. Like that makes it less scary somehow. I don't know. All I know for sure is that I didn't say anything. I just let her go.

A few hours later the cop showed up. He said she crossed the centerline on I-77 and ran straight into an oncoming semi-truck. He asked if she'd been drinking.

"No, no," my father had said. His voice was tight, controlled. He was keeping it together for my benefit. But he began to shiver. "She never drank. Maybe half a glass at Christmas." His voice broke, and he turned away, a deep sob wracking his shoulders.

I remember thinking that the sound of my father crying was the most horrible sound on earth. It terrified me. Crushed me in an instant. I put my arms around him and held tight.

"She didn't crash because she was drinking," I said to the cop. "She crashed because of me."

I SHAKE OFF THE memory and focus on the drive. I head straight to the place I've gone to a million times before: Jay's house. I skip the front door because I haven't used it since the ninth grade. Jay always lets me in through his window. I mean, there's no reason I can't use the front door. Even late at night. His mom is usually out on a date with some weirdo she met on the Internet. But his bedroom is on the first floor, so his window is like my personal VIP entrance.

I peer through the window and there he is, lying on his bed in his favorite T-shirt, blue with gold lettering: Go W.H. Bees. That's our high school baseball team—the Woodhull High Bees. And I guess small, stinging insects are an appropriate mascot for a sprawling Ohio high school that combines two suburbs of Cleveland. I mean, our sheer numbers make us a little menacing, but still, you could kill us with a flyswatter. Or a can of Raid.

His baseball shirt is the same one he wore the day we sat on my front porch steps when I first opened up about my mom, about how guilty I felt. He seemed to get it right away. Jay told me his mom had never been that good at being a mom; I told him mine had never been that good at being happy.

I reach up to knock on the window but stop. I'm so afraid to tell him why I'm here. I stand there, sort of paralyzed, and watch. He's propped up on some pillows, staring at his glowing iPhone screen. His guitar leans against the bedframe, and on the wall behind him are several posters: Pink Floyd, Led Zeppelin, The Doors. When we first met, I asked him why he listened to old music.

"Simple," he'd said. "I like it because it kicks more ass."

I remember smiling and thinking, *I'm so into him. How could I not be totally into him?*

I take a deep breath and tap on the glass.

He jumps off the bed and sweeps his hand through his thick brown hair. "Hey," he whispers, cranking the window open. "What's up?" He holds my hand as I climb up to the windowsill and jump down onto his soft blue carpet.

"Hey." It's all I can manage, like I'm drowning in the awkward silence and can't choke out any more words.

"Talk to me," he says. "You don't look so good." His pale brown eyes glimmer as he studies me the way he always does when he's worried—with that if-I-can-fix-it-I-will look. And I want to tell him everything, that I saw Mom, that I think I know why, but I freeze, suddenly all too aware of what a nut bag I'm about to sound like.

I think I saw my mother today. I want to find her. And I think you can help. And I always tell you everything . . . Well, everything but the whole I'm-into-you thing. But, this. THIS. I can't think of a way to tell you THIS.

"I'm fine," I say, stalling for time. "Just a little stressed."

"About what?"

I wildly search my mind for potential stressors in my life that do *not* involve seeing someone who died two years ago. *My room's a mess. I think I overheard my dad flirting with some woman on the phone, and it made me want to hurl. I'm worried because I haven't gone up a bra cup size in, like, forever.*

"You're not worried about the history test are you?" he asks.

History test. Perfect. I used to be a straight-A student and ace everything from history to biology to physics. After Mom died, I just couldn't focus. Or care. Or even remember why I used to care.

"Yep, I'm a mess over it. Who *is* Polk, anyway? Keeps me up at night."

"Nice use of the Henry Clay campaign slogan," he says with a grin. "Well done. Very hard to do in casual conversation." He reaches up to give me our traditional greeting: a fist bump followed by the opening of our hands in a little fade-away motion. It's sort of lame, but we saw it in a movie once and decided it was the perfect greeting—especially when you're me. After Mom's funeral, it didn't take long to get sick of the pity on people's faces when they saw me, followed by one of those it-sucks-to-be-you hugs. So Jay and I decided we'd do the fist-bump handshake at all times—good and bad—to protest the world's proclivity for pity-you greetings.

"I'll help you study tonight," he says. "No worries, we'll—"

The sound of a gong and crashing waves interrupt him.

"What the hell?" I ask.

He flops onto his bed and grabs his cell phone. "Got a text," he says. "It's my new notification noise: Zen bells."

Whoever it is makes him smile. He even laughs a little as he types back. I crawl onto the end of the bed and lean against his footboard. In my head, I'm running through different ways to tell him about seeing Mom. *So, I was at the store today. No. So, you know that cross that's in your living room? No. How do you feel about life after death? NO.*

Jay texts away, his eyes shining in the bright screen light.

"Anyone ever tell you that your eyes are the color of diet maple syrup?" I ask. He shakes his head no, but doesn't look up. His fingers keep pecking at the screen. "Just wondered. And I'll be right back. Going to the bathroom," I lie.

"Okay," he says, still not looking up.

I slink off the bed and head down the hallway. But instead of going straight for the bathroom, I take a detour into the living room. In the dark, I can see the sofa and walnut end tables with matching brass lamps. I imagine Jay's mom bringing her myriad dates in here for a middle-aged romp on the pristine white cushions. The thought makes me feel vaguely ill, but mostly it pisses me off. Jay's mom is so messed up. There should be some rule that before you're allowed to have a kid, you have to prove yourself. You have to know how to handle certain major life stuff that gets thrown your way: death, life detours, disappointments. I don't know what the test would be exactly, but you should have to pass it with *at least* a 70 percent.

I walk around the sofa and click on one of the brass lamps. On a long skinny table next to the window is a glass case I've seen a million times before. I peer inside. A tarnished silver cross necklace sits on a little velvet cushion. It's all scratched up and engraved with what I think is a Latin word. *Magis.* But I have no idea what it means. A brass placard sits next to it. SAINT IGNATIUS OF LOYOLA, LOST CROSS, CIRCA 1556.

Jay's dad was Howard Bell, a well-known theology prof up at Case Western. To hear Jay tell it, he spent his entire life (including parts that might have been better spent with Jay) studying the works of an old Catholic saint named Ignatius. His dad had been obsessed with finding The Lost Cross of St. Ignatius—last seen in the 1500s—ever since Jay was a baby.

That he actually *found* it made Jay's dad sort of famous. But the discovery fueled his drinking. Jay says people think all alcoholics wear dirty raincoats and drink booze out of paper bags under bridges. It's not true. There are all kinds of alcoholics—even super successful smart professors who think if they just drink at home at night after all the kids go to bed they aren't hurting anybody. Late one night when Jay was about ten years old, his dad polished off nearly a whole bottle of scotch—the drink he called "the intellectual's comrade"—and fell down the basement stairs. His head struck the concrete floor. Jay found his body in the morning in a dried puddle of blood.

I shake off the image of little-boy Jay finding his dad. It's just so awful. I look back down at the cross in the glass case and read the print etched into the glass.

DO NOT TOUCH.

Yesterday, that's exactly what my best friend, Kate, and I did.

I HAVE THREE BEST friends total—Kate, Jay, and Noah. And we hang out at Jay's all the time, mainly due to his mother's nearly guaranteed absence. I call them "best friends" even though that stupid label doesn't come close to describing what they are to me. There really isn't a word in the English language for it. I met them freshman year in the after-school tutoring/counseling program we were forced into called Back on Track. The four of us were sent there because we all had two things in common: our once-stellar grades were in a death spiral and our attitudes were those of aspiring screwups. We were all budding failures at life, but the four of us bonded for an entirely different reason.

Most kids landed in Back on Track due to typical stumbling blocks: too much pot, too much booze, too much pot *and* booze, or too much undiagnosed (enter favorite psychiatric condition here). But not the four of us. No, ours was both weirder and more tragic: all of us had someone close to us die. There was Jay's dad. There was my mom. Then there was Noah's brother, Cam, who hung himself in their basement three years ago. And Kate's aunt—who was like a mother to her—was killed by a violent ex-husband.

And unlike the baseball team, the Woodhull High Back on Track program doesn't have a T-shirt. But if it did, I'm guessing it would feature our school's bee mascot, wings shackled, wearing a dunce cap and sitting next to a honey jar—full of Prozac.

The tutoring and the counseling haven't helped our grades all that much or even our outlooks on life, but I know we've learned something about loss: when you find friends who know it, who've been through it, who really, really get the ache that moves in and lives in your bones, it gets a little easier. And the things you share with those friends, the things you know about them and what they know about you, makes the term "best friends" a complete and total joke.

So yesterday, while Noah was at a dentist's appointment, Kate and I went to Jay's without him. When Jay picked up his guitar and was about five songs deep into amateur Pink Floyd hour, Kate and I took a break and started roaming the house. That part wasn't unusual. Other than the fact that Noah wasn't with us, we typically have to bail when Jay feels it necessary to play "Wish You Here" in a loop. What *was* out of the ordinary was what we did. The kitchen offered the usual snacks that ranged from canned beans to moldy pecan sandies, so we made our way to the living room to watch TV. But when there was absolutely nothing on, Kate went over to the glass case with the cross necklace inside.

She later claimed that boredom drove her to pick it up and that her typical clumsiness caused her to drop it on the floor. The bottom cracked and the locked case broke open.

Without thinking, without even talking about it, we both

tried on the cross. She went first. I don't know why, really. I guess we were just curious; we wanted to touch something that old. And even though it sounds crazy, I'm thinking that maybe wearing this cross made me see my mom. That maybe it's cursed with some sort of Catholic voodoo or something. Maybe that was why it was so important and valuable to begin with, why Jay's father went to all that trouble to find it.

I peer in at the necklace again. I shake my head because my idea is *nuts*. I don't believe in any of that spiritual stuff, anyway. I've never bought what religion is peddling—that there are super special people that the Pope has decided to call "saints" who have direct tickets into heaven, or that there's some Big Dude in the sky who gives a rat's ass about my tiny little life. But if I'm wrong, and He *is* Up There, then He's not exactly someone I'm interested in friending. You know, for that whole letting-my-mom-get-in-a-car-wreck-and-die thing. Somehow, I just don't think we'd really hit it off that well. Too much water under the bridge.

But then I find myself talking to the silver cross. Even though I don't *really* believe it's any more special than the BFF necklace I won out of the Big Grab machine at the mall when I was ten. I don't believe it at all.

"If you made me see my mom," I whisper through the glass case, almost angry, like a hiss, "then make her come back."

WHEN I GET BACK to Jay's room, he looks up from texting.

"Everything come out okay?" he asks with a snarky smile.

"Gross," I say, flopping onto the bed beside him. I take a deep breath. "So, I have a sort of weird question for you."

"Okay. Ask it."

"It's about that necklace. The cross. The one your dad found. Have you ever—"

His phone gongs and, just like before, the room fills with the sounds of crashing ocean waves.

"Whoa," he says. He starts texting again, his maple syrup eyes all bright and happy. "Give me a sec. Have to write back."

I feel like a loser just sitting there, so I take my phone out of my pocket and stare at the textless screen. It doesn't help. So I Google stuff about St. Ignatius and his cross. I get links to information about the order of priests he founded called the Jesuits and all sorts of Jesuit university homepages. And I try to absorb the information, but I can't. Big surprise: I run into that whole focus problem I've had since Mom died. The words just sort of run together.

Jay is still texting away, oblivious.

I Google phrases like "seeing the dead" and "dead people sightings" and "cursed crosses." The hits are all over the place. Groups pop up: Wiccans, medicine men, fortune-tellers, ghost whisperers. A link to a pop-psychology article about people who claim to have "the gift." I try to read it, but it's insulting. Anyway, I get the gist. Apparently people who tell their therapists that they've seen or interacted with the dead "can't accept change" and have a "juvenile wish for things to be different or better." *Wanting your mom not to be dead is juvenile?* Whatever. I skim ahead until something grabs my attention: "Many patients report seeing the dead at their gravesites."

The cemetery. Of course.

I give Jay a gentle nudge on the thigh. "I need you to come somewhere with me. And we sort of need to go—like, *now.*"

"*Okaaay,*" he says, still not looking up from his phone. "Do I get to know where?"

"Can I explain on the way?"

"This is highly weird," he says, still tapping the screen. "But I'm intrigued."

"So you'll come?"

He finally quits texting and frowns at me. The frown says it all.

As if you even need to ask.

Chapter 2

Love Sucks.

The cemetery is about fifteen minutes south. A little shorter if you take the interstate, which I do. I can't stop thinking how crazy this all is, that I'm driving to my mother's grave to actually *look* for her. And Jay's phone is still blowing up with text messages. Every other second the car fills with gonging and wave crashing. It's driving me nuts.

"Who the hell *is* that?"

"Nobody," Jay says, still typing. I don't like that answer. *Nobody* means *somebody* that you're not naming for a reason. But whatever, we're at our exit.

I take a left off I-77 and begin the drive toward the cemetery.

"Wait," Jay says. "Where *are* we?"

"Nowhere," I answer. (Two can play that game.) I just keep driving. Finally, we reach the entrance and stop, the huge stone sign in my headlights: RICHFIELD CEMETERY.

"Oh, Riley," Jay says. "I had no idea we were coming here." He puts his cell in his pocket. "I thought you were worried about the history test. But you're . . . missing her?"

"You could say that, yeah," I say. "We'll have to climb over." I point at the giant padlock and chain wrapped around the gates.

I pull the car into the grass and park. We get out, and he quickly scrambles up the iron fence. I follow more clumsily and get stuck at the top, the sharp pointy tips gouging my leg through my jeans. Jay grabs me before I fall and helps me down. He gently sets me in the grass, not letting go until he's sure I have my footing. I look in his eyes, then at the bright, pinprick stars all around us, and for a moment the night actually seems sort of beautiful. But then I remember where I am and why we're here. "Beautiful" isn't really the word I'd use to describe this night. Or any part of my life, really.

We walk toward the graves in the darkness, and a breeze passes over my skin like the brush of cool fingertips. We each grab our iPhones, using the flashlight apps to illuminate the path in front of us. Jay looks on edge, his eyes a little wide as we slowly drift among the headstones and flowers people have left, the fake blossoms looking tattered and faded in the cold iPhone light. We make our way around trees—pines, big old oaks, weeping willows like silhouettes of frozen fountains. I hear a rustling and the snap of a twig.

"What was that?" I whisper. In a mad rush, I find myself sweeping my phone around looking for my mother's light blue sweater, her floral print dress, her eyes.

"A squirrel," Jay says behind me. "Nothing to be afraid of."

My nerves jangle, but I turn back to the path. "Sorry. Graveyard at night. Dislike."

When we reach her flat marble stone, I feel like I always do—like she's been missing and I've just stumbled onto the first sign of her, the first real trace of her, something tangible that reminds me she was real, that having a mother wasn't just some cruel, distant dream. I fall to my knees and rub my hands over the letters.

CLAIRE WALKER STROUT
1968–2011
Wife, mother, daughter, friend.
Loved and missed, but in our hearts forever.

Jay has been with me more than a few times when I've done this. And as always, pain blooms in my chest, strong enough to bring tears, strong enough to *need* tears, but none come. I never cry. Not since we buried her. I just—can't.

Mom, where are you? I saw you. I know it. Please, come back. Just one more time. Let me see you one more time.

And I wait. I wait to hear footsteps in the grass, her laugh high and lilting among the pines, to see the flutter of her dress behind another headstone. I breathe deep, trying to catch the smell of her lavender perfume. I don't know how long I sit there like that, but it feels like ages. Just waiting, listening, looking. Above all, hoping. But there's nothing. She's not here.

"Talk to me," Jay says, placing a hand on my shoulder.

"I'm sorry . . . I guess it's nothing," I say, trying to convince myself. I turn to look up at him. "Nothing but that—I miss her. I really, really miss her."

He gives me a melancholy smile. "Then why are you apologizing?"

THE DRIVE BACK TO Jay's house is quiet. And awkward, at least for me. I feel so unglued. I can't believe I dragged him to my mother's grave so late at night. Freshman year, I could have explained this away. But now? He must think I'm crazy, forever broken. *Maybe I am.* The silence is interrupted by the gong and crash of the Zen text noise. I think I'm grateful for the distraction. But my eyebrows arch, asking again.

"Okay, okay," he says. "It's Sarah Larsen."

Hot Sarah? Popular Sarah? Lost-her-virginity-at-like-thirteen Sarah? I stare at the road, numb. She's the ringleader of the worst group of girls at our school, the girls who embody everything that's bad about a predominantly white Midwestern suburb like Brecksville. They're Cleveland-is-scary girls; they call Akron "*Crack*ron." I mean, Akron has admittedly gone downhill since Goodyear shut down their tire plant, but still, you don't have to be an asshole about it. "Tell me you're not going to ask her out. She's obnoxious, vapid, totally conformist. How you can you be into someone like that who—"

"She's actually pretty funny," Jay interrupts.

At least he's not texting back. I mean, we just visited my *mom's gravesite*—to sit there and text would be a level of jackassery heretofore unknown. He reaches down and silences his phone.

I know I really shouldn't be all that surprised about Sarah. He always goes for the wrong girls. Like the time he fell for the president of the Honor Society, who didn't even know Pink Floyd was a band. When he played a gloomy song of theirs on guitar for her, she started laughing. Or the time he went for this super-jock girl who was an all-star W.H. Bees volleyball player. She suggested they go on a run for their first date. Try as I might, I couldn't get the smile off my face when he told me that he nearly hyperventilated in the first quarter mile. Needless to say, neither relationship worked out. It's like Kate always says: *His picker's broke.*

"We have a lot in common," he adds.

Like you both need oxygen to breathe?

"Whoa, what's that face about?" he asks. "Careful, wouldn't want it to get stuck like that." He says it gingerly, like a question: Is it okay to joke now?

I force an it's-all-good smile as we pull up in front of his house. "Thanks for coming with. I just . . . needed to go."

He looks at me for a second, sizing me up, trying to tell if it's really okay to let me drive home.

"I'm fine," I say. "Just need to go to bed. Get my rest. I have a history test *and* a physics test to fail tomorrow."

That convinces him, and he opens his car door.

"Night," he says, his brown eyes catching a sparkle from the streetlight above. He reaches up for the fist-bump hand-shake.

"Night," I say, our hands gently touching. *Ask him. Now.* "Hey, Jay?" I say it before he has a chance to shut the passenger-side door. "Weird question for you."

"Okay. Shoot."

"You know the cross necklace your dad found?"

He nods.

"Well." I pause, realizing how deranged I'm about to sound. "You ever, like, wear it?"

"You're right, that's totally weird. You know that my dad always handled it. Threatened to kill us if we even touched it. It's like a million years old. Why?"

"Did *he* ever wear it?"

"I have no idea. I mean, he always kept it locked up. But, seriously, why are you asking?"

Now he's looking at me like I'm a total freak, and I know I need to come up with some sort of reason why I just randomly brought it up.

"I saw one of those antique shows on the History Channel,"

I lie, though I'm not sure why. I could've worked the cross into a real explanation somehow. I could've asked if Jay ever missed his dad all of a sudden, at weird times, like I missed my mom tonight. If the feeling was ever so strong that it made him do strange things, like try on that cross. After all, the necklace helped kill his father. Jay has said as much: People became a lot more forgiving of his drinking after the discovery. But Sarah Larsen threw me for a loop. "You know, the ones where people pawn all their parents' heirlooms for cash? Made me think of the necklace, that's all."

After a moment, he shrugs. "Yeah, well, it would be the douche move of the century to pawn it. I keep telling my mom it should go to a museum." His face softens, but he still doesn't look convinced that he shouldn't be worried. "You *sure* you're okay?"

I nod, and he looks directly into my eyes, studying me.

"Okay, then," he says. "Goodnight."

"Night."

He takes a few steps toward his house but then stops and slips his cell out of his back pocket. *He's texting Sarah back. He can't even wait until he gets inside?*

In my mind, I run through the sad emoji list on my phone. I think of the crying ones and the variety of tear placements on their faces. A sad face with a single tear on the right. Or on the left. Above the eyes or below? A face with a stream of tears on both sides. I move on to the handful with varying degrees of frowns and no tears at all. But even with the vast array of sad choices, none really fit.

I imagine what the I'm-having-hallucinations-about-my-mom emoji would look like. Its face would be confused, a lost look in the eyes. A tiny bottle of meds would be open next to it, a stray pill rolling away. I imagine what the

I-am-completely-and-utterly-depressed-because-I'm-into-my-best-friend emoji would look like. It would be unsteady on its feet, on the verge of vomiting, holding a sign that says LOVE SUCKS.

And that's exactly what I text Jay. Maybe because I'm losing it, maybe because I saw my mom, maybe because I feel like the whole world is coming apart, but I text him:

LOVE SUCKS.

One, two, three. He looks up and turns. He walks back to the car, opens the passenger door.

"What?" he asks. "Love sucks?"

I can feel a hot blush overtaking me, like I'm trying to hide the fact that I was just stung by a hundred bees. He stares at me, waiting for a response. As each second ticks by, I come no closer to inventing some sort of reasonable explanation for why I just texted him LOVE SUCKS. I stare at him blankly.

"Riley," Jay says, his brown eyes shining. "Why'd you text me that?"

And just as I feel like I'm going to break, that I'm going to open my mouth and tell him everything, that I saw Mom, that I'm so into him—it happens. As quick as a breath, I catch a glimpse of something—or someone—right where Jay is standing. I scoot back, press myself against the driver's side door. But it happens again. In and out. Like my eyes are failing me, losing focus; I see flickers of blond hair and hazel eyes.

"Hang on," he says. He looks down at his cell and texts away. My lungs lock up, refuse to draw a breath, but I manage to put the car in drive.

"Okay, done," he says. I don't look at him. I've got my eyes pinned on the little gnats swooping in and out of my head-light beams. I can't look over at Jay; I just can't. "Sorry, I just felt like I *had* to text Sarah back," he says. "What were we talking about last?"

"I, I—" I stammer.

"Oh, right: love sucks. Why'd you text me that?"

My mind won't work. *Say something.* "Just don't get too wrapped up with the wrong person. I've done it and it sucks, that's all."

"Who? And when? You've never had a boyfriend—"

"Someone you don't know," I lie, manufacturing an imaginary person. I manage to look at him; he seems normal now, but totally confused.

I can't stay there one second longer. I put my foot down on the accelerator, the passenger door still hanging open. I leave Jay standing by the curb, in the dark. I don't even look back in my rearview mirror. When I get about ten blocks away from his house, I realize I'm speeding. I nearly run a stop sign and slam on the brakes. The car comes to a screeching halt, halfway in the intersection. I look up at the jumble of stars in the sky, my heart bursting, racing.

What's happening to me?

Chapter 3

You, Too?

I crawl straight into bed when I get home, pulling the covers over my head like I did when I was a kid, hoping the outside world will disappear if I can't see it. I huddle over my cell like it's a tiny, warm campfire. But instead of popping and crackling wood, I hear the pings and jingles of incoming texts. Jay asks if I'm okay, if I got home. I stare at the blazing blue messages, unable to write back.

But finally, slowly, my fingers start to move over the keys. I manage to convince him that I'm all right, that I'm just missing my mom, that I'm stressed about the tests tomorrow. He doesn't ask again why I texted LOVE SUCKS to him earlier. I kind of wish he would, because right now, in this blanket-tent, after this day . . . I just might tell him.

For the next few hours, I stare at the glowing plastic stars on my ceiling and count sheep, telling myself this is all a bad dream. I can't get much higher than 300 bleating, fluffy, maniac sheep jumping over a fence before I have to start counting over again. Somewhere around sheep number fifty, they all take on an evil, sinister look.

You're nuts, they say as they propel themselves over a section of white picket fence. *Resident.* Jump. *Of.* Jump. *CRAZY TOWN.*

AT ABOUT THREE IN the morning I decide to head to the kitchen and get some milk. I don't really think milk is going to be strong enough to deal with whatever psychotic break it is I'm having, but it's worth a try. I grab my cell and turn on the flashlight app to light my way down the hall. But then I see that Dad's light is on in his room.

I quietly make my way to his door and peer in. He's in bed reading with the covers tucked neatly around him, the bedside lamp casting a soft, sad glow on his aloneness. He sees me and flashes one of his I-swear-I'm-happy smiles that I can see right through. Then I see Mom's favorite Sleepytime Tea mug on her bedside table. She always had a cup before bed. I wonder how long it's been there, if I've seen it there before and not noticed.

"Mom's cup," I blurt out, pointing.

"Oh," Dad says, glancing down at the mug with the picture of an impossibly comfortable-looking bear in a nightcap on it. "Huh. I guess I put it there and forgot? Sometimes I put things of hers on her side. Makes the room feel a little less empty."

What's that noise? Oh, right. That's my heart. Breaking.

Seeing the sadness in Dad's eyes, seeing Mom's mug on her bedside table as if she set it there to steep and will be back any minute to take a sip, I nearly lose it. I can feel it rising in my throat, this *need* to shout, *I SAW MOM, I SAW HER.*

But I shake it off. I can't tell Dad about this; I never tell him anything but the good stuff, the I'm-fine stuff. I always try to fly just under his radar. And I know that's sort of sad or lonely or whatever, but when you're the kid who wrecked everything, the kid who ruined her mom's life and then caused her death, your personal philosophy goes something like this: *Sit down, shut up, and try not to take up too much air. You've caused enough trouble already.*

"I was on my way to get some milk. Want some?"

Dad nods and gets out of bed. But when we get to the kitchen, he doesn't go for the milk. He goes for the skillet.

"Eggs?" he asks.

"At 3 A.M.?" Dad looks disappointed that I'm about to turn him down. So I backtrack. "I mean, yes. Eggs. Sounds awesome." I attempt an I-heart-eggs smile that I hope looks real.

He smiles, too, and his blue eyes shine like freshly lit gas burners. He picks up his spatula and fires up the stove. I don't know why I was shocked that he wanted to make 3 A.M. breakfast. My dad communicates through his food. It's not that he's terrible at talking to me; he actually does a pretty good job. He bites the bullet every once in a while and asks me about embarrassing things—boys, school dances, my plans, my hopes. But it's hard for him. What comes easy is the cooking.

"Why can't you sleep?" he asks, as he cracks an egg against a bowl.

I'm crazy. Paranoid. Freaking out about a cross necklace. I must be dying. Brain tumor. Something.

"Nothing," I say.

My father doesn't respond but gives me "the look." He started giving me "the look" after Mom died. It always makes me feel like the stuff we smash between little glass slides in biology and then shove under a microscope. Or like one of the houses he inspects for damage. That's part of what my dad does for a living: he works for a real estate company and appraises and inspects houses before people buy them. He checks out the roof, the plaster, the foundation, looking for defects only the trained eye can see. The more damaged the house, the less it's worth.

Now, he peers at me like that, like he's studying the insides of my brain, looking for hidden areas of damage or disease. I try to act normal, like everything's okay, but I wonder if he can see the cracks in my foundation.

"I'm *fine*, Dad," I lie again. "Just tired."

He gives up on the inquisition for the moment and goes back to cooking. I can tell he's whipping up what he calls a Special Plate Breakfast. He finishes the eggs, cuts wheat toast down the middle and covers it with butter and blackberry jam. He softly whistles as he puts fruit on the side, a grapefruit already cut into little wedges. I smile and know that each egg is a word, each wedge of fruit, punctuation. They don't actually spell anything, but their meaning is crystal clear: *if I could fix your heart I would.* My father and I share the same blood, the same loss, the same wish to fix each other, and the same sadness that we can't. And sometimes, we both just drift around the house like two rainclouds trying desperately not to storm. But as he proudly sets my Special Plate Breakfast down on the table in front of me, I see it—through his deep, dark sadness, I see his hope for my life, I see his love for me glimmer in his eyes like sunshine glinting off a windswept lake. *If only you and Mom had never had me. She'd be here, alive, healthy, happy. I wasn't worth it. This breakfast should be for her.*

"Great eggs, Dad," I say. "They're perfect. Really perfect."

He smiles then puts some eggs and toast on a plate for himself. I wonder what he'd say if I told him that I saw Mom.

The first time I can remember running to him with really big news was when I was five years old. As I was bathing, I noticed something I'd never noticed before. I jumped out of the bathtub and ran down the hallway trailing bathwater behind me.

"Dad!" I screamed.

He was in his room buttoning up a favorite red flannel shirt.

"Look!" I said, pointing down. "I'm growing a penis!"

My mother had not explained to me that my anatomy was as it should be and would not be getting any bigger. My father looked at me, his soaking wet daughter, who thought she was growing something only her dad would understand, and searched for a response. I was expecting him to be stoked, celebratory. Instead, he crossed his arms over his chest and smiled at me nervously.

"Well, blow me down," he announced.

And then he walked away.

That night, he made my favorite homemade pizza—pepperoni and ham with the ideal 3:1 pepperoni-to-ham ratio. I ate the pizza, but I was mad. How could his only response to my news be *pizza*?

Now as I sit in the kitchen, eating my perfectly cooked eggs, bursting at the seams to tell him what happened, it occurs to me that I am still that little girl—the one who ran to him with all her big news that she needed him to explain. What dish would he prepare in response to hearing that his daughter thinks she saw her dead mother? A soufflé? A pork loin, perhaps? Maybe three-cheese vegetarian lasagna—complicated with *a lot* of layers.

"Are you sure nothing is wrong?" Dad asks as he takes a bite of eggs.

Don't tell him. Don't do this to him. He needs you to be okay.

"What's wrong is that you're a shift-eater," I say, trying to steer him off topic, knock him off the scent of my sadness. "It's annoying. Live a little."

"A what?"

"A shift-eater. You eat in shifts. One thing at a time. Currently, you're on the egg shift. Next, you'll move on to the toast." He tries not to, but he smiles again. *Mission accomplished.*

IN THE MORNING, I drive myself to school as usual in my red station wagon—which is not sporty, racy, or really that awesome in any way, shape, or form. Plus, I'm pretty sure it's the official car of the forty-something, risk-averse crowd. Dad bought it for me because he thinks it's the safest car on the planet, and I guess as cars for high school kids go, it's not all that bad. My friends have decided its pet name is the Dragon Wagon.

I wheel into the school parking lot and scan the front lawn, looking for my friends among the mass of students. I don't see them right away. Woodhull High is ridiculously huge. This is what happens when you cram the 'burbs of both Brecksville and Broadview Heights into one school. All the buildings on the sprawling campus are painted in blue and gold; plus there are multiple baseball fields, tennis courts, soccer fields, and a football stadium, all adorned with the W.H. Bee, fists up, wings back, stinger nowhere in sight.

Finally I spot Jay and Noah near a small elm tree, so I make a beeline for them (no pun intended), coaching myself as I go. *You will not see your mother. You will not see anything out of the ordinary. This is the Midwest. Only boring things happen here. Just breathe. And try to be normal.*

Noah is talking, and he looks upset. His blond hair is disheveled, and he's waving his arms around. Plus, he's wearing what appears to be a soaking wet T-shirt. It's a classic Noah shirt. It's NASA blue, which matches his eyes, and has a fake periodic table on the front with only three elements: Ba, Co, and N.

"Hey," he grumbles at me. He turns away from Jay and wipes his shirt with a McDonald's napkin. "You wouldn't happen to have any spare nerdy science shirts, would you?"

"Um," I say. "Maybe in the car?"

Noah goes back to looking super upset, yet I still laugh. I can't help it. Because Noah always makes me laugh or smile. It's like his job in our group; we all get bummed about something, and he'll read the situation perfectly and figure out a way to make us feel better. Plus, he's an awesome friend. On the first anniversary of Mom's death, he blew up my phone all night with texts; he could tell I wasn't okay even though I said I was. None of us had a license yet, so he got his mom to drive him to my house even though it was almost midnight. I opened the front door and there was Noah, holding a bunch of flowers in his outstretched hand. They were wildflowers— long and ratty-looking wildflowers with clumps of dirt still hanging from their roots.

I found out later that he tried to buy roses at Heinen's, but they were closed. So he made his mom pull off on the way to my house so he could pick wildflowers from the side of the road.

Crazy, I know.

"So how did you manage to get the whole fake periodic table wet?" I ask.

"Unbelievable. So I'm standing by this tree," Noah says, pointing at the trunk. "Waiting for you guys. Enjoying my amazing biggie Coke. The perfect healthy start to a school day." The faintest grin appears on his face. "And all of a sudden Carl comes down out of the tree."

"What?" I ask.

"Yeah, I know; right?" He runs a hand through the honey blond mess on top of his head. "The bastard climbed up there just to mess with me, and then swang down and knocked my Coke out of my hands. It went all over my shirt." He points at the ginormous wet spot as if it's not amazingly obvious to begin with. "But the worst part is that all I managed to call him was a shithead. Very unsatisfying."

I consider correcting Noah's conjugation of the verb "to swing," but decide against it. His incorrect usage does not alter the fact that anyone who purposefully swings down from a tree to knock a drink out of your hands definitely deserves to be called much more than a shithead.

"Sorry, Noah," I say. "That sucks."

There's a group of kids at W.H. who apparently live to torment us and anyone else who is decidedly uncool. And Carl is one of them. They do stuff like that to us all the time—they steal books out of our lockers, post Facebook crap like *Riley and Kate made out in the locker room, picture unavailable.* They even put bologna and eggs on the Dragon Wagon to mess with the paint. And yes, Kate and I *did* spend an entire gym period hiding in a shower stall together to avoid the dodge ball tournament; however, no making out ever occurred. Kate got hit in the boob the last time we played and has suffered the nickname Boober ever since. So instead of choosing to suffer, we dragged a couple of stools into the shower stall and sat reading Twitter on our phones. It was lame, but way better than dodging a large inflated rubber ball for an hour to cries of "Boober in the rear! Boober in the front!"

Noah peers into his biggie Coke cup to see if any is left. "I swear I'm going to beat the crap out of that guy one day."

Jay and I opt to nod sympathetically rather than say what I know we're both thinking: *yeah, right.* Noah has his share of muscles, but they're the long and lean soccer-guy type—not the beefcake, trunk-of-a-tree kind like Carl has. My money would have to be on Carl in a fight. But of course there never will be a fight, because Noah in fact has a brain, unlike Carl.

I grab a few of the McDonald's napkins out of Noah's hands and try to help. I'm smiling again and Noah is smiling now, too, at least. We both know idiots like Carl will torment us until graduation day; it's guaranteed, like having to take the SATs. Best just to laugh it off. But out of the corner of my eye, I catch Jay watching me, sizing me up, gauging if I'm really okay after I drove off like a maniac last night.

"Let's walk," he says to me. "We've got ten minutes before the bell."

I can't look at him. I'm worried I'll come unglued again. I can *feel* what he's thinking—*I know you aren't okay, Riley. Start talking.* And I'm just so tired. So damned tired. I can't talk about any of this right now. I just—can't.

Fortunately, the fourth member of our little dysfunctional clan shows up next. Kate's iPod earbuds are jammed in her ears, and her gorgeous black hair is tied up in an unruly knot on her head.

"Who you listening to?" I ask. I eye her iPod, trying to see if it's a new one. Kate was thrown into Back on Track because she responded to the death of her aunt by stealing her mother's credit card. (In addition to failing all her classes, like the rest of us.) She bought everything from new five hundred dollar boots to a stupidly expensive purse. And she's still doing it. She "borrows" cash or her mom's card on a semi-regular basis. She claims it's a compulsion, and maybe it is. You have to watch her like a hawk.

"JUDDS," she says way too loud. "AND DON'T WORRY, THE IPOD IS OLD."

Jay reaches over and gently takes her headphones out. "You're screaming," he says. "And listening to country music. Those are two very serious early-morning violations around here."

"Whatever." As she tucks a stray strand of hair behind her ear, I look for any signs that she's about to lose it, too. We both tried on the cross, and if my hypothesis is right about some weird Catholic curse, then she'd be seeing strange things, too. But she looks totally normal and decidedly un-freaked-out. "My aunt Lilly was originally from Kentucky," she says as another piece of hair escapes from her disorga-nized bun. "And she always said that down there the Judds are considered honorary colonels."

"Honorary colonels, huh?" I ask. Kate nods. I don't know what that's supposed to mean, but I can tell I'm supposed to be impressed—so I am. "Well, I guess I'll have to give the Judds some more thought," I say.

Kate smiles and heads for her first class. Even though I know I'd rather be dragged behind a herd of wild horses than be forced to listen to one note of Kate's music, I don't want to hurt her feelings. I make it my general policy in life not to be an obnoxious ass, and am continually surprised by the number of people who seem not to share this goal.

"If I'm ever captured by terrorists, there could be no greater torture than if they strapped me to a speaker blasting the Judds singing 'Bridge Over Troubled Water' on a loop. I hope they don't know that," Noah says.

"Don't be an ass, Noah," I say. "Let's go in, already."

He shoots me a quizzical look. "Whoa. What's up with you this morning? You okay?"

Apparently, I can't fool Noah either. He knows me too well. He knows something's off.

"Yeah, I'm good," I lie.

"No, you're not," Jay says. He peers at me with his typical sincere concern that makes my insides lurch with a mash-up of feelings.

"I'm *good*," I say again. "Fine. Just about to fail a history test *and* a physics test today, that's all."

"No, that's not all. Why'd you drive off like that last night? Are you sure you were just . . . missing your mom?"

"Yes. Yes, I was—I am. Now, take me to physics or lose me forever."

I BOMB BOTH TESTS. I still know exactly zero facts about James K. Polk, which as Jay pointed out last night makes Henry Clay's "Who is Polk?" campaign slogan especially poignant for me. There was no way I could cram when I got home from the cemetery. I try to focus harder when I get to the physics exam but bomb that in an equally spectacular fashion. I try not to think about my mom or Jay as I read word problems about fulcrums and the surface tension of water rising in a capillary tube. I pray for a C. I try to remember what it was like before Mom died, when I did all my homework and actually studied. But I can't. It's like my ability to care died right alongside her, and I have no idea how to resurrect it. I mean, you can't just order up motivation like it's a Happy Meal or something.

Whatever. I fill in all the blanks.

AS SOON AS I get home from school, I crash on my bed and take a nap. I wake to the sound of my dad calling me for dinner. I rub my eyes and realize I feel a little better. A little more stable. *Must have been some sort of freak-out yesterday. Maybe some delayed grief.*

I stand and stretch, glancing down at my cell as I pull on my favorite sweats.

Jay has sent me about a million texts.

WHERE R U?

WHERE R U?

WHERE R U?

WHERE R U?

WHERE R U?

WHERE R U?

I start to text him back and ask what's up, but before I can send a message, I hear the doorbell. I run downstairs and open the door.

It's Jay. And he looks like he's dying. His skin is somewhere between peach and lime green. Instinctively, I take his hand and lead him up to my room. My dad lets us hang out in there as long as we keep the door open. He worries that a closed door means we're in a lip-lock, which provides a great example of the lesson that *most* of what we worry about will never happen.

"What's wrong? You're shaking," I say as I try to sit him down on my bed.

He won't sit. He just keeps pacing.

"I. I. Oh my god." He runs to the bathroom and leans over the toilet. I follow him and rub his back. I'm briefly distracted by the smell of his skin mixed with the scent of man-deodorant. I think they put hormones in that stuff. Good ones. I run my hand over his shoulders. They have muscle definition but avoid the extremes: They aren't bony but they also don't have that fake, built-in-the-gym look. *Snap out of it*, I tell myself. I glance down at my abdomen, about where I think my ovaries are. I don't know if it's anatomically true or not, but I blame them for what is currently coursing through my veins. I imagine them as egg-shaped cheer- leaders, obnoxious and misguided, tossing pom-poms in the air and chanting a cheer about Jay and getting n-a-k-e-d.

"Do you have the flu?" I ask, trying to focus on anything but the way he smells and the way his warm back feels under my hand.

"No."

I feel his head; it's ice cold but sweaty.

"Something you ate?"

"No," he says, moving away from the toilet. We walk back into my room and sit down on my dark green carpet. "Just promise me you won't tell anybody."

"I promise."

"I mean, really. You can't tell. Not even Kate."

"Okay, okay. Just tell me. Go."

"I think I'm crazy," he says.

"You're not crazy."

"Riley, I saw my dad today."

My heart feels like it freezes, stutters to a stop. He waits for me to respond. I can't.

"I know, I know, but I swear I saw him," Jay says in the silence. "Sitting on a bench by the river. I was walking the dog after school and went right by him. I tried to shake it off, thinking it couldn't be him. But I couldn't keep going. I had to stop. I stood about twenty feet from him and just—watched. It was my dad, I know it."

"Did he see you?" I ask, when I'm finally able to speak.

"Yeah, he saw me and—"

"Recognized you?" I ask.

"Yeah. Instantly. And—"

"And as soon as he recognized you, he was gone?"

Jay stands up and looks at me like I'm possessed. "How did you know that? How did you—"

"Because it happened to me." *And I think something happened when I was looking at you, too.* But I don't tell him that part, I just tell him about seeing my mom. We talk a mile a minute, over each other mostly, as we compare stories. At first, Jay thought he was seeing things. Before he saw his father by the river, he thought he saw a person who was a woman one minute, but when he turned, she was a kid, a little girl. But he shook it off—until he saw his dad.

Jay walks me through the whole encounter. Just like my mom, Jay's father was in the outfit he was buried in. He wore his nice suit and blue tie. His dad was sitting there, half-smiling like he was praying or meditating or something. Jay said he was gazing out at the muddy Cuyahoga River that flows through Brecksville.

"He was so still and calm," Jay says. "From his face, you'd think he was staring at the Pacific Ocean at sunset or something. Not like my dad at all. To be calm like that. I looked right at him, and as soon as he recognized me, he was gone. And I was looking at someone else. Someone I've never seen before."

I must look as sick and unsteady as I feel, about to pass out, because Jay puts an arm around my shoulders. Just then, my dad appears in the doorway. He stiffens up when he sees Jay holding me. We pull apart.

"I wanted to tell you that dinner is ready," Dad says. He looks at the floor.

"Hello, Mr. Strout," Jay says, nervously tugging at his shirt. "Good to see you. I was just—"

"We were just talking," I blurt out. "About some stuff."

"Good to see you, too, Jay. Feel free to stay and eat." Dad doesn't look up. Blushing, he turns and heads back downstairs.

"Awesome," Jay says, exhaling. "We just medaled in synchronized awkwardness."

"Whatever," I say. "He always thinks we're—" I stop, too embarrassed to finish my sentence. The reality of all this hits me hard—*Jay saw his dad; I saw Mom.* I can tell there's a look in my eyes that's never been there before. I can feel it; it's something like—hope. "Maybe they're out there, Jay."

"What?"

"Our parents. Maybe we can find them—"

"Whoa," Jay says. "You're crazy pale. Just breathe for a second, okay?"

He takes my hand and leads me to the front porch. We usually don't hug. The closest we get is our usual fist bump. But Jay steps closer and puts his arms around me. I don't know what to do, so I just go with it. I rest my head on his shoulder and look out at our yard. It's dusk and the lightning bugs take turns lighting up the trees, like long strings of tangled and twinkling Christmas lights. The crickets chirp all around us, like soft sundown alarms that parents all over town have set and hidden, timed to go off all at once and remind us to come home.

"I have something to tell you," Jay whispers. I pull back a bit and look into his eyes, asking but not sure I want to know what more there could be to this story. "I know it's crazy, but the Saint Ignatius necklace, the cross, I—" he stops.

I finish his sentence for him. "You wore it?"

"Yeah," he says. "After you left last night and you asked me about it, it hit me that I'd never even touched it. My dad always threatened to kill us if we did. But I went home and picked it up. Then I put it on. Just for a few seconds." Jay pauses for a second, disbelief filling his eyes. "You don't think—"

"Yeah. Because I wore it, too," I whisper. "One night when you were in your room—"

"I figured that's why you asked," he says. I nod. He pulls me close and we're silent for what feels like a few centuries. "It'll be okay," he finally says, even though I know he doesn't believe it. "We'll figure something out."

I squeeze him tighter and close my eyes, willing him to stay here, to not change, willing this all to go away. He squeezes back and then gently lets me go.

Chapter 4

Me, Three.

I spend my second sleepless night in a row trying to doze off but jumping awake at every noise: a rush of wind, a barking dog, a distant train whistle. I fight the urge to check under my bed and in my closet for—what exactly I'm not sure—and fail. I shine my iPhone on the contents of my closet, pass it over all the shoes, terrified I'll see someone behind the hanging clothes. I get on all fours and lift up the dust ruffle around my bed and scan the dust bunnies to make sure no one is there.

I stare at the ceiling and wait for daylight. When it comes, I finally doze off. But my eyes pop open at 9 A.M., and I drag myself out of bed, thankful that at least it's Saturday, and I don't have to face school. I walk to my chest of drawers to search for a T-shirt, but then I sit back down in the middle of the floor in my pajamas. I feel like an earthworm flushed out onto the sidewalk by a heavy rain, stuck to the pavement, drying out by the second.

I stare up at the ceiling again, at my red and white plastic balloon light. It's been there since I was a baby. And by my bed is a puppy lamp. The base is a resin dog looking at me with impossibly large tear-filled eyes. The lampshade is painted with a pile of puppies all tumbling over each other in a ridiculous romp of joy.

Maybe it's time for this stuff to go.

My mom and I had big plans to redecorate my room. I used to go through magazines and describe the images out loud to her. We'd gotten as far as picking out wallpaper, but then—the accident.

A knock at my door breaks my train of thought.

"Phone's for you," Dad says as he peeks his head in the door. "It's Kate. Says she tried your cell but you weren't answering." I can't cope with the thought of talking to Kate and listening about her latest crush, or listening about anything for that matter.

"I put it on silent," I whisper. "Just tell her I'm sick. Can't talk."

He tells Kate I'll call later and hangs up.

"You really feel sick?" he asks.

"Sort of."

He puts his hand on my forehead and a serious look passes across his face as he focuses on reading my temperature. "Nope. Cool as a cuke," he says way too happily. I don't understand why a cucumber is considered colder than any other vegetable, but I figure he likes it because it's a food analogy, so I never call him on it.

"Dad, there are all *sorts* of illnesses that don't cause fevers," I protest as I crawl back into bed.

"Like what?"

"Like . . ." I pause, my mind going blank. I retreat to the safety of food. "I feel like an overcooked hardboiled egg. You know, when the shell cracks a little and the white stuff kind of oozes into the water. And the yolk gets all dry in the center."

"Oh," he says, finally looking concerned. "So your head *and* your stomach?"

I nod like crazy, even though I don't have a clue how he got a headache and a stomachache out of what I just said. "Yeah. Stomach and head. Real bad."

"Well, I'll start some Jell-O. If you're sure . . ." he pauses searching for words. "That you're just a little sick."

"I'm fine," I say, pulling the blankets over my head. *And by fine I mean so absolutely far from fine I couldn't even see fine if I had a telescope.*

"I just think that—" Dad is cut off by the ringing phone. "Oh, dammit. Hello? Yes, here." Dad pulls the covers down and hands me the phone. "It's Kate again. Says it's urgent." I roll my eyes and put the phone to my ear.

"Hey." All I hear is crying. "Kate?" I sit up.

"You've got to come over here," Kate chokes out between little sobs. "I'm freaking out."

No, no, no.

I stare at my Dad. He stares at me. The phone feels cold against my ear. "Kate," I manage. My tone is much calmer than I would have expected. "Who'd you see?"

The crying immediately stops.

"How did you know?" she asks.

"Just tell me who you saw."

"Aunt Lilly."

We all know Aunt Lilly. She's the reason Kate ended up in our group. She's been dead for almost two years.

I TELL KATE I'LL be there in five minutes. My father's eyebrows arch in that I-thought-you-said-you-were-sick kind of way.

"It's urgent," I say to Dad as I text Jay and Noah. I tell

them to meet me at Kate's house ASAP. "Girl stuff. Let me go? Please?"

Dad shakes his head, clearly debating with himself whether or not to push me on this, to find out what's really wrong. But *girl stuff* almost always succeeds in scaring him off. "Fine," he agrees after a minute. "But be back for dinner. I'm doing a fantastic pot roast. With garlic mashed potatoes."

"Okay," I say as I rifle through my drawers, looking for a clean T-shirt. "It's a deal."

Dad sighs and hesitates, but then goes downstairs while I shower and change. I put on the shirt and jean shorts, run a brush through my wet hair, and head down to the kitchen. I take a few deep breaths on the stairwell to hide the panic that's building in my veins so Dad doesn't get upset. But one line keeps running through my head over and over: *It's happening to all three of us.*

"Oh, I forgot to mention the parsnips," Dad says as I enter the kitchen. "Really great rosemary roasted parsnips."

"Parsnips?" I manage a smile and kiss him on the cheek. "Wouldn't miss those for the *world.*"

I head out the backdoor and cross the yard, proud that I kept it together in front of Dad. I put a foot on the stone wall at the edge of our property, grab onto the branch of a dogwood tree and pull myself over. The wall is covered with ivy, and I have to make sure my sandals don't slip on a waxy green leaf; I've had countless skinned knees jumping over this wall on my way to Kate's.

The reasons I've jumped the wall on my way to her house have varied since we've been friends. Sometimes it's major, like when she found out that her dad had a not-so-secret girlfriend. Other times, it's more minor, like when she thinks her mom has imposed an unfair punishment over whatever her latest credit card debacle is. Or like when I feel the need to have a meltdown over the fact that Jay is a moron who will apparently never get that I'm in love with him. We cope by eating huge bags of Cheetos. Or lying on the grass in her backyard, staring up at the stars. We talk about how life really makes no sense if you think about it. How some people die early. How some people don't.

And then there was the gum episode. I totally lost it on Mother's Day sophomore year. Kate told me to come over to her house after school, and when I got there, she'd bought crazy amounts of gum. All sorts. Orange dreamsicle gum. Key lime pie gum. Gum in cubes. Sticks. Balls. Pink. Blue. Even purple. She had sugar-free and the kind that's so sweet the sugar crystals make your tongue raw. We sat together on the floor of her bedroom surrounded by mounds of it. And I felt so weird because I just couldn't cry, so she cried for me—and we chewed and chewed and chewed. And I told her the thing that scared me the most was that it still hurt so bad sometimes I couldn't talk about it. I couldn't find words.

"When the gum wrappers reach knee height," she said, in her I'm-totally-serious tone, "then we might find words. We might begin to process. But not now. Not before the gum."

And she was right. Words did come to me after we made it through the pile, and I was able to tell her: *Thanks for being awesome.*

This is the thing between us: we stick together no matter what. No matter how much she gets on my nerves or I get on hers. And I know she's freaking about seeing Aunt Lilly. But at least I know exactly how she's feeling. I go as fast as I can toward her house, fighting to keep my balance while I walk along the retaining wall that goes across our neighbor's backyard. Still I break into a run when I see the giant willow tree in Kate's backyard. It's like an enormous green shroud, the greatest tree to sit under, the first place Kate retreats to when her parents are mad or when she's depressed. Just as I expected, she's sitting on the ground, leaning against the thick trunk.

Even in the soft sunlight filtering through the leaves, she looks pale and sickly. I sit beside her. Her usually shiny black hair looks dull and limp. We just look at each other for a moment, as if we're both watching, studying each other's faces, looking for some irregularity, something out of place that would signal we're both in a dream. I reach into my pocket.

"Gum?" I say, holding out the pack. Since the gum episode, I never go to her house without it; it's our medicine. She nods, and we both take a piece. We unwrap them in silence and start our ritualistic chewing.

"How'd you know?" she asks between loud chomps. Tears fill her eyes.

"I saw Mom. In the grocery store. And Jay saw his dad."

The chewing stops.

"Don't panic. You'll swallow the gum." I decide against telling her what happened with Jay the other night as well. "Just breathe. And keep chewing."

Reluctantly, she blows a bubble. "How are you even calm right now? How are you so good at this?"

"Good at what?"

"Being all leader-ish. And chill."

"I didn't know I was," I say. And I don't. All I know is that when someone-I care about is panicking, I get calm and start saying things I don't believe like *it'll be okay,* and *everything's fine.* Plus for the past two years, it's like I can't *really* panic or really *feel* much of anything. When a real feeling starts, it gets cut off at the pass with a wave of numbness.

"Well," Kate says. "I guess this takes the struggling montage to a whole new level."

That's what we always say when nothing's going right. We tell ourselves that our lives are movies, and in movies there's always a huge part of the story where the heroes struggle like hell to make it to the happy ending. Bad guys have to be fought off, girlfriends have to be wooed back, records have to be set straight—and then there's one big hellish montage before it all works out, right before the credits. It's where we are right now, but I can't even smile at the joke. I've never been less sure of a happy ending.

"I hate this movie," Kate says after a moment. "I mean, I expected scenes like getting dumped or having horrible parents. But I didn't expect a *seeing-dead-people* scene."

"Well, I have a theory," I venture. "But I'm guessing it will freak you out even more."

"Um, I really think we've reached freak-maximum here. I don't think there's anything you could say that would—"

"You know the million-year-old silver cross necklace at Jay's house?" I ask before she can finish. "The famous one that belonged to Saint Ignatius?"

She stops chewing. "The thing in the case? By the sofa?"

"Yes. That. The one we wore Wednesday night?"

"No way," she says slowly, shaking her head. "You think?"

"Yeah," I say. "Jay put it on for the first time, too. Then he saw his dad the next day. When did you see Lilly?"

"OMG, I thought I saw her Thursday." She starts chomping again, animated. "Like, I caught a glimpse of her in the Target parking lot, but when I looked closer it wasn't her. I shook it off and just thought it was someone who looked like her, you know? But then this morning, running errands for my mom downtown. I saw her. I *know* it."

We hear the gravel crunching beneath Jay and Noah's feet as they come up the driveway.

"Holy Catholic crap," Kate says, her eyes wide. "Should we like, call the Pope or something?"

"Yeah, you have his cell number?" I mutter.

Finally, I am able to get Kate to smile.

THE FOUR OF US head to Kate's basement, our usual spot the rare times we hang out at her house. It has baby blue shag carpet and fake wood paneling along the walls. There's a green/orange carpet stain right at the base of the stairs that belongs to Jay. During a particularly egregious game of Truth or Dare, we dared him to drink a mixture of raw eggs and Mountain Dew. Juvenile, I know. He kept it down for about thirty seconds.

Kate flops down on the mustard-yellow corduroy couch. I sit next to her and the guys sprawl out on the floor in front of us.

"So what the hell is going on?" Noah says running a hand through his blond hair. "I am not cool enough to have more than three friends. And all three of you look like you're losing your minds. This leaves me alone in the world. Unacceptable."

As usual, he's trying to keep it light, but it's obvious that he's really worried. I can tell by the way he's looking at me. Noah has mastered the tell-me-everything look; it's impossible to keep anything from him. Not that the four of us keep any secrets from each other, anyway. But still, that look is like his superpower.

"Seriously," he says, "this better be a real emergency because my new coronagraph just got here. And I was just about to try it out when Jay called me and told me to get over here."

"Oh no," Kate says. "Please don't explain what a choreograph—"

"It's a *corona*graph, and it's *amazing*," Noah says, lighting up. "It fits over the telescope and blocks out direct light from the sun when you're looking straight at it. So you can see really cool stuff in the sun's atmosphere that you wouldn't be able to see without one—"

"Wake me when he's finished," Kate interrupts dully.

"Oh, come on," I say. "Let's not be all anti-knowledge like a bunch of popular douche bags." But really I'm just trying to postpone the inevitable, because it means I'll have to relive the moment when I saw my mother.

"I'm with Kate," Jay says. "Can we please shelve astronomy and figure out what the hell is happening here?"

"By all means," Noah says. "Go. It just better be good."

Jay describes what happened, how he saw his dad by the river. Summoning my courage, I explain in a rush how I saw my mother looking at bubble bath in the grocery store. Kate, clearly drained, chimes in last about her Aunt Lilly. She shivers as she speaks. When she's done, we look at Noah. He looks at the floor.

"So, Captain Normal. You see anybody?" I ask him, forcing a smile.

Noah slowly shakes his head no. "Are you all serious right now? Like, this really happened?"

"Yes and we're doomed," Kate says. "It's so end times."

Kate is always saying that. We even joke that it's the name of her movie. If her dad and her mom make it through a whole day without fighting, it's a sign of the end times. If she scores more than 70 percent on a math quiz, if three pairs of shoes she likes go on sale simultaneously: end times. Until now, I've always rolled my eyes. But even *I* can agree that when your friends start seeing dead people—TOTALLY END TIMES.

"I know what I saw," Jay says, getting a faraway look. "It was him. It was my dad. And he was meditating or something. Calm. He'd never just go sit by a river. Not in a million years. Not without a martini, anyway."

"Mom was doing something she'd never do, either—picking out bubble bath," I say. "She wouldn't even allow herself to stay in bed when she had the flu, let alone soak in the tub just for fun."

Kate nods in agreement. "And I saw Lilly in the storefront of the Fountain Hobby Shop, where they offer painting classes. *And she was taking one.* Lilly would *never* take a class. She was the original Southern Lady Colonel. She couldn't stand to be told what to do."

"What the hell is a Southern Lady Colonel?" Jay asks. "Sounds kind of hot."

Kate rolls her eyes. "Do you people know *nothing?* An SLC is a totally feminine, proper woman. *And* a ball-busting-take-no-prisoners badass at the same time. To master that combination is an art form. I'd like to think I'm one."

"You've never busted balls," Jay says, ruffling her hair. "Not even one single ball. Ever."

"This is ridiculous," I say, standing up. "Can we *please* stay focused? How the hell did we get onto southern gender norms?"

"Seriously," Noah says. "I mean, I know *you're* being serious right now, so we have to figure this out. There has to be a logical explanation. What have you all done together in the past few weeks? Did you eat bad food or something? Didn't you all have that disgusting fried fish at Yorkshire Fish 'n' Chips? That's definitely bad enough to cause hallucinations."

"It's *not* the fried fish, Noah," Kate says. "It was—"

Three rapid-fire gong sounds—from Jay's phone—cut her off.

She frowns as he fumbles for it. "Text emergency?" she asks.

"God, it's probably Sarah again," I say.

"*Sarah Larsen?* No way," Kate says with a wicked grin.

"Yeah," Jay says, concentrating on his cell screen. "I think she's into me?"

"Oh, Jay." Kate sighs dramatically. "You are *such* a lost soul. She wants a history tutor, not a boyfriend, honey."

Noah scoots over to the couch and sits by Kate's feet. "Forget Jay. We have to figure what you guys saw."

"Just tell him," Kate says. "It's because we wore that evil, cursed—*thing*. Ugh, I can't even say it out loud."

"Whoa, hold up," Noah says. His eyes are wide, attentive. "Wore what?"

"She wore it, too?" Jay looks up from his cell. I nod.

"We both tried it on that night at your house," I say. "When you were in your room playing "Wish You Were Here" on a loop."

"Um, hellooo?" Noah says, waving his arms around like he always does when he's rattled. "Would someone like to fill me in? Wore *what?*"

"The Saint Ignatius necklace," Jay says, jabbing at his phone. Apparently he can flirt with Sarah Larsen and still participate in our conversation and collective freak-out. What a multitasker. I find I am annoyed with him, and not just because I'm jealous of Sarah. "The cross. The old one my dad found. All three of us have worn it. "

"You tried it on?" Noah says slowly. A weird look passes across his face; I can't place the emotion, and Noah, like all of us, is pretty transparent. "But it was locked up. In the case."

"Maybe we're just nuts," Kate mutters. "I mean, the necklace can't *actually* have caused this. This is *real life*, not Lord of the Rings."

"Dude," Jay says, eyes still on the phone, now waiting for a response. "The Lord of the Rings wasn't about *the actual Lord*. Jesus and the saints had nothing to do with that. If that's what you were going for, your metaphor doesn't hold."

Noah scowls at him. He doesn't notice.

"Whatever," Kate huffs. "Since you're besties now and all, can you text Sarah for me? Tell her I'm sick or something. She'll know what it's about."

Jay finally looks up. "What are *you* texting her for?"

"Just do it, okay? Long story."

He shrugs, but starts jabbing at his screen again. I shoot a look at Kate. *Why on earth do you have a "long story" with Sarah that I don't know about?* She looks down at her nails really fast and acts like she doesn't see me—but I know she does.

"Um, Sarah says to tell you that you HAVE to come," Jays says after a second, his eyebrows twisted in confusion. "In all caps."

"Come where?" I ask.

Kate looks stressed. "You guys will kill me if I tell you. Can you just come with me to school really quick?"

"No way," Noah says, pacing again. He comes dangerously close to pacing across the old Truth-or-Dare stain. "We need to go to Jay's and get the cross. If you all wore it, then—"

"I'll go with Kate," Jay says. "I wouldn't mind saying hey to Sarah . . ."

Great. I'll go, too. I can watch Jay flirt with his new crush and

watch my best friend cavort with her awesome new best friend . . .
Sounds like a real picnic. I feel my fingernails dig into my palms
as I seethe on the couch. *Meanwhile, we seem to have conve-*
niently forgotten that three of us have suffered HALLUCINATIONS.
Yes: ALL CAPS FOR EMPHASIS, SARAH LARSEN FANS.

"Wait," Noah says, giving Kate a be-reasonable look. "Can't
we at least go get the cross first? And I'm not going to school
with you unless you tell us what's up."

"You'll understand when we get there," Kate replies
uncomfortably, her cheeks regaining some of their color.
"Then we'll go get the cross. Okay?"

Noah sighs but nods.

"What's our plan if we see them again?" Jay asks. His voice
is quiet. "If I see my dad—I don't know if I can handle it."

"At least we'll all be together when it happens?" I say,
working hard at being the cool one, the leader, like Kate said
before. Like I do all the time. Like nothing can penetrate
the numbness. But it hits me hard—the thought that I could
see my mom. Deep inside somewhere, I feel the tiniest belief
that she's alive. The thought is a tickle at first, but then it's
an ache, then a vice-like grip. I worry I'm going to throw up.

"Hey," Noah says, noticing. "You all right?"

Even though I've said *I'm fine* so many times in my life it's
my own personal mantra, I don't say it. I don't say anything,
least of all the truth:

No. Not okay. Not okay at all.

Chapter 5

Working Theory

The school auditorium is in total pandemonium. People are everywhere: gathered around a huge Gatorade cooler by the door, up on stage practicing what looks like a choreographed dance, sitting on the backs of the blue and gold seats in the audience, and running up and down the aisles. Some are in jeans, but some are in full workout gear.

"No way," Noah says as we walk in. He nudges Kate in the arm. "You got invited to be on the *air band* team?"

Kate nods in shame. No wonder she was embarrassed to share this with any of us.

Every year our school has an annual air band competition among the grades. It is exactly what it sounds like, and exactly as lame. Basically, the popular kids run the thing, select who'll be in each air band, select the songs that will be blasted over the speakers, and then the rest of us get to watch them make asses of themselves as they pretend to be rock stars, but with no props and no talent. It's ridiculous. But the fact that Kate has been asked to join means she's been invited to ditch us and move up in the social ranks.

"I love that they have a Gatorade cooler," Jay says dryly. "Like air band is a sport."

"Fake singing and fake instrument-playing are super dehydrating," Noah says in an equally deadpan voice. "Throws off the electrolytes."

"I just want to know when leg warmers made a comeback," I say.

But even with the wisecracks, I can tell we barely have the energy to be all jokey-jokey. We're all on edge. I can't handle being in a crowd right now, and I'm generally not claustrophobic. We get who-invited-them looks as we go. I feel like even more of a total freak. I can't stop looking around, terrified I'm going to see my mom, yet part of me desperately wishing that I will.

"Can you just find Sarah and get going with this?" Noah asks Kate. "I want to get out of here ASAP."

"Jay and I'll go look for her," Kate says absently, scanning the crowd. Jay doesn't protest. My jaw tightens as I watch them head off toward the stage, but I keep silent.

"Let's sit," Noah says. "Take a break? You're not looking so good, Riley."

"Gee, thanks. People are saying that to me a lot these days."

"You know what I mean."

We slump down in a couple of empty seats. I take a deep breath and stare at the ceiling. I don't want to see Jay get all googly-eyed when he finds Sarah, and I don't want to see Kate launch into a full-scale suck-up. Noah leans forward and checks his cell.

"I hate to be a downer, but I miss my brother's texts," he remarks out of nowhere. "I mean, they were always weird and super dark. But funny sometimes, too. In that dark comedy kind of way."

I shake my head. "You're not a downer. I totally get it. Missing weird stuff like that. I miss the way my mom would always make some really funny comment just when she was finished crying. Her eyes would be all red and puffy, but she'd be smiling. I mean, it was sad, you know? But her jokes were always funny as hell."

Noah shoves his cell back into his pocket. "Can I ask you a question?"

"You have to ask permission?"

"Do you *really* think you saw your mom?" he whispers. "And it was the day after you wore the cross, right?"

I shrug. "Yeah. It was the day after. And I thought maybe I just hallucinated the whole thing. You know, like I was just having some sort of crazy grief thing, thinking I saw her. But how do three people all hallucinate the same thing? I mean, how can that be just a coincidence? Part of me really thinks that I saw her—that she's alive or . . ." Or *what?* I stop, getting lost in all the improbabilities. I look up at the stage, as people run back and forth looking for their places. I'm terrified to look too closely, terrified they'll get that blurry look, that I'll see different people flicker and flash in their places. Maybe even Mom.

"I chickened out," Noah says. He's checking his cell again. "Just now. That wasn't my real question."

"Well, you *have* to ask now."

Noah slips his phone back in his pocket for a second time and smiles, his hair falling in his eyes a bit. I catch myself noticing why the band and theater girls are so into him.

"Why do you like Jay so much?" he asks.

He knows. Backtrack. Fake it. Hide it. Funny. Be funny.

"He's a friend. I like him for the same reason I like you. I don't have any other options." I look at the floor, hoping he'll drop it.

"No. You *like* him. I can tell. It's the way you look at him, even just now in Kate's basement. I can see it in your eyes," Noah says. "Why? What is it about him?"

It's my turn to do the cell routine now, pretending to check for texts. I feel so exposed. Did Kate blab, or is it really just obvious? Am I that loser friend that everyone feels sorry for? Am I pathetic, but no one has the heart to tell me? I don't *feel* pathetic. But maybe that makes it worse—the truly awkward never know they're awkward, *which just makes them more awkward.* Maybe I should give up on lying. I suck at it, apparently.

"Does he know?" I ask.

"No. And that's kind of my point. It just seems like if a really awesome girl likes you, and you can't even see it, it's just—what a waste."

"GO!" Sarah calls from the stage. She's in the leg warmers I'd just protested, tights, and a ripped-up T-shirt. Her getup reminds me of this old '80s dance movie I saw on TV. She moves her hips to the right. "Right!" she calls. Then to the left. "Left!"

The group behind her mimics her moves. They shake their hips, practically hump the air, twirl around, and then do some sort of god-awful sexy (at least I'm guessing) crawl move on the floor. The music is loud, and it's a horrible pop song. From what I can tell, the whole thing is about the importance of being hot. And willing to make out with . . . everyone.

"Really? Is there even a guitar in this song? Who does air band without air guitar?" I ask, avoiding Noah's eyes.

The words "awesome girl" hang in the air between us. I'm awesome? I mess with my phone again. If I hadn't vowed to avoid Twitter for the rest of my life, I know what I'd tweet:

Awesome girl? #defineit.

But I don't tweet, and out of the corner of my eye, I can tell Noah is looking right at me. Finally, I give in and look up from my phone.

"I don't get it," he says.

I can tell we're not talking about pop music choices.

I like Jay. That's all I can say. He gets it and he gets me and I can't help myself. When he's around, it's just—there.

"Well," I start, searching for words. "He knows what it's like to lose a parent and—" I feel bad as soon as I say it. Like losing a parent is worse than losing a brother.

"Oh I get it," Noah says slowly. "So that's it. It's the exclusive Jay and Riley Club. The rest of us don't *really* understand."

I look down at my sandals and my unpainted toenails. Loss is loss. I shouldn't compare mine to Noah's or to anyone else's. But just as I'm about to apologize, Noah cuts me off.

"Just don't wait on Jay too long, that's all," he warns, but his tone is gentle.

He gets up and gives me a look that's somewhere between sympathy and Riley-you're-so-clueless. Then he walks away.

I lean back against the blue velvet auditorium seat and watch him go. I want to call him back, to ask him what he means, ask him how he knew, ask him how lame I am on a scale from one to ten. I start to say something but chicken out. Mindlessly, I play with the mute button on the side of my iPhone, flicking it on and off with my thumb. Mute. Unmute. Mute. Unmute.

My spiraling thoughts stop when a girl in a red sequined flapper dress costume catches my eye. She's standing in a group of Sarah Larsen's cronies by the stage, swishing the old-fashioned hem around her legs, tossing her head back and laughing like she's just heard the funniest thing in the world. She looks like she's straight out of *The Great Gatsby*.

Like it's 1929 and she's off to drink a vat of bathtub gin to soothe the pain of the great stock market crash. *Why the hell are people in costumes for air band? Are they doing a 1920s take on current/awful pop music? That makes exactly zero sense.*

I look down at my phone and silently beg for a text message to come through so I can have a distraction. But my phone sits silently in my hand like a dead fish—a dead, incredibly unpopular fish. I look back up from my cell. The flapper girl looks frustrated now. She's not laughing anymore. It hits me that I don't recognize her at all. And Sarah's group is not big enough for me not to know . . .

And then, with the thump of a single heartbeat, she's gone. Her red sequin dress, her cute bobbed hair, her long string of beads—all of it vanishes. And in her place stands a girl I *do* know. It's one of Sarah's main "buffers," the crew of slightly less good-looking girls that Sarah keeps around her as a human buffer zone to protect her from the onslaught of incoming suitors. I blink and blink again. But the flapper girl is nowhere to be seen.

I stand but keep my eyes on the auditorium floor. I'm too afraid to look up, scared of what or who I'll see. *Walk. Just walk. Just get out of here.* But it's hard to walk through a crowd when you're staring at the ground. I keep bumping into people and mumbling a half-hearted "sorry" here and there. But I can't look anyone in the eye.

It's only when I reach the hallway that I can finally breathe. For the first time in my life I'm actually grateful for the rush of air from lockers-full-of-who-knows-what smells. I'm relieved to be out of the auditorium, out of the crowd, but then I realize that I'm running. I tell myself to slow down, to just walk, because now I *can't* breathe again. I pass classroom after classroom and force myself to read the labels by the doors to try to slow my brain down—biology, history, Spanish. My heart still pounds, and I catch myself peeking into my calc class, peering inside, half-wondering, half-hoping that I'll see my mom sitting in a desk chair, scribbling in a notebook with a pencil, or writing equations on the marker board in her beautiful handwriting.

But I see nothing. Just empty desks, piles of math books on a shelf, a trash can full of candy wrappers and Doritos bags.

I'm almost to the exit. But then I stop. In front of the principal's office. Because there, on the floor, leaning up against a glass display case full of sports trophies and school artifacts, is Kate. And she's crying.

I kneel down beside her, put an arm on her back.

"Whoa," I say, gasping for air, my own lungs heaving. "Slow down. Breathe. What happened?"

"Idiot," she squeaks out and then wipes her face with her arm. "Total. Idiot."

"What did I do?" I ask her.

She gently laughs and looks up, her face puffy and red, black mascara streaming down her cheeks. She's in full-fledged ugly-cry mode. "No," she says, her eyes softening. "Not *you*. You're awesome." She sniffles again and leans into me. I gently push a strand of her beautiful black hair behind her ear before it gets covered in snot and tears.

"Then who's the idiot?" I scoot closer to her. Her head falls on my shoulder.

"Me," she says. "For thinking they could actually want me in air band. I walked up to Sarah and her friends. And they told me that they just wanted me to come so I could be their *water girl*. One bee-otch even told me to go to 7-11 and get her some Corn Nuts. Ranch flavor. To 'keep her strength up' for her dance routine."

I look up at the stained foam ceiling tiles. *High school. What a cruel last stop before adulthood.* "I'm sorry," I say, wishing I could line them all up outside and tell off every single one, or better yet, magically turn them all into non-asses. "They're awful people. They really are—"

"But that's not it," she says, her voice getting smaller. "Carl was there."

"Well, we all know he's the worst one."

"No, listen." She sits up straight, looks right at me. She seems so scared all of a sudden, almost panicked. "He wasn't Carl the whole time. When he started saying stuff to me about being the water girl, he . . . changed. Just for an instant. He was this boy I've never seen. In old-fashioned clothes: brown burlap pants, this old thick cotton shirt. Like off that old show, *Little House on the Prairie* or something." She stops, and the tears start again. "And then he was Carl again."

I can't think of anything to say. My throat closes up; my mind goes blank. I want to tell her about the flapper girl, I want to tell her this is real, I want to tell her that I'm so scared, that I don't know what's happening to us, that I have *no idea* if we're going to be okay.

"It'll be okay," I say, feeling the normal wave of numbness take over. "Let's get out of here."

Outside, the afternoon air is hot and humid. It's almost summer break, and the sun on my skin feels so good. My mind drifts to normal summer days—heading to the pool, eating frozen Snickers bars, accusing Kate of stuffing her bikini top. What I wouldn't give to have a summer like that again.

I text Jay and Noah and tell them to meet us outside ASAP. Kate and I sit on a giant boulder by the school's massive flagpole to wait, our backs touching. I can feel what she's thinking. *This is totally end times.* And I'm thinking she's right.

"What happened now?" Noah says as comes out of the school doors. Jay is right behind him.

"We're getting rid of it," Kate says.

"Pardon?" Noah asks.

"The necklace," she says. "The Saint Ignatius cross necklace. We're going to get rid of it."

Jay's eyes get wide. "Did you guys see . . . ?" he stops, unable to finish. I nod.

"Not my mom," I say. "But yeah. Kate and I both saw these people, like, old-fashioned people . . ." but I stop, too. I just can't say any more out loud.

"I'm in," Jay says. "This is going to drive us all crazy. Let's go get it and just destroy it. Or throw it in the river or something."

"But we can't," I say slowly, softly. "Maybe it's the only way to my mom."

"I'm with Riley," Noah says. "We're *not* throwing a priceless religious artifact into the Cuyahoga River."

Kate gets up, but then sits back down. It looks like fainting is imminent. "I'm freaking, I'm really freaking," she says. "I mean, what if we aren't the only people this is happening to? Maybe *everybody* is seeing what we are, and it has nothing to do with the necklace. And maybe everyone is afraid to say something about it. Maybe the zombie apocalypse is starting, and we're just the first to know."

Miraculously I sort of laugh. Only Kate or Noah could make me laugh at a time like this. "I *don't* think this is the zombie apocalypse. But there's an easy way to test it out." I spot a fellow nerd coming out of the school. Her name is Jackie. She plays the trombone, and she has on a long-sleeve T-shirt that says TREBLE MAKER.

"Jackie?" I wave her over.

"What's up?" she asks. "Can you believe they picked a song without guitar in it? I mean, seriously. *Why* the school forces us to go watch this is *beyond* me." She rolls her eyes.

"Yeah, super lame," I say, gathering my courage. "Um."

"Yeah?" she looks concerned now because I'm acting so awkward.

"Um, have you ever, like, seen someone who's died? Like, seen a glimpse of them?" I ask. *This must sound so absurd.*

"What?" she asks, clearly taken aback by the absurdity. She pushes a strand of frizzy brown hair behind her ear and looks at me like I'm a total asshole.

"Like a ghost. But not a ghost. Have you seen someone who's already died, like either they faked their death, or maybe they're back from the dead? And then you go to talk to them and they turn into someone else?"

Her face goes from confused to angry as she backs away from me. "Have you gone to the dark side? You're picking on people now? What's your problem?"

"I'm not trying to mess with you, I promise . . ."

But she's already walking away. Then she gives me the finger. That makes twice in one week that someone has felt the need to flip me off. Can't really blame them in either case.

I turn back to my friends.

"I think it's safe to say she hasn't seen anything," Noah says. "If it's any consolation, Riley, I can relate."

I laugh again, miserably this time. "Yeah. I think it's just us. The ones who wore the necklace." My mind whirls, trying to make sense of something that is senseless. "Maybe . . . I don't know. Maybe we should leave this to the experts. Let's go get it and take it up to the archeology department at Case

Western or something. Where Jay's dad was a prof. Maybe they can help us."

"Sorry," Jay says. "I'm still in the ditch-it camp."

I don't like the sound I hear in Jay's voice. Like something's broken, or missing. "Don't you want to figure this out?" I ask him.

"I don't know," Jay says softly. His eyes are on the ground. He bends down and picks up a small stone. Then he pulls his arm back and throws it as hard as he can. We watch it arch high in the sky and come down near the big pine tree. "I just want to get rid of it. Get rid of all of it."

"Okay," Noah says. His voice has an edge. "I'm empathizing here, I really am. I get that this is sad and awful. But really, I'm so annoyed with you all, I'm going to have to put all my reasons in list form." He starts pacing again like he did in Kate's basement. "One: The cross necklace is like, *old*. It's like, an *artifact*. It took Jay's dad's *whole career* to find the thing—it does *not* belong in the river or a dumpster somewhere. B: We *can't* turn it over to the university. They'll take it from us, but they won't believe us or help us. Three: I'm starving, which doesn't help."

I decide it would be unwise to point out that Noah started his list with a number and inserted a letter halfway through. Jay and Kate roll their eyes at Noah's speech and take off toward my car.

"Wait," Noah calls. "Hang on." They stop and look back. "Before you go, before we decide on anything, let me run into the computer room and at least do some research. My phone will be too slow here. The service sucks."

"Research on what?" Jay asks, sounding fed up.

Noah pauses. "On our options. I mean, if it is some sort of crazy Catholic curse, and we're going to destroy the necklace, we need to make sure we do it the right way. So all this really does stop." Noah pauses again, gauging our reactions. "And if we're going to ask somebody up at Case Western for help, shouldn't we know who to go to? I can research some profs. Why don't you guys go get some food and bring it back here so I don't pass out from hunger? I'll meet you in the computer room."

Jay narrows his eyes, pondering Noah's idea.

"I actually think it's a good plan," I chime in. Of course, I'd say anything to buy some time, to prevent Jay and Kate from taking off to get rid of what might really, truly, crazily be a means to connect to my mother. "If we're going to do something, let's at least get it right."

After a long moment, Jay nods. But he's still glaring at Noah. "Fine," he says. "Taco Bell?"

Noah sighs in relief. "Seven-layer Burrito. Times two."

I GO WITH JAY and Kate to make sure they don't convince themselves to pick up the cross on their way. Taco Bell is all the way in North Royalton, which takes like ten minutes to get to. Everyone behind the counter moves so slowly, we can only assume they're all stoned. But still, we make it back to the school in about thirty-five minutes.

The sounds of air band practice echo down the hallway as we head to the computer lab, loaded down with food. A knot pulls tight in my stomach; I don't want to look into the gym as we pass. I don't know who or what I'll see. We duck into the computer lab.

The room is full of gently humming hard drives; the walls are covered with posters about learning to code. Yellowed laminated charts about Pascal, Fortran, and C++ stare down at us. But other than that, it's deserted.

"Where is he?" Kate asks.

I peer under the desks, just to make sure Noah isn't sneaking a nap or looking for something he dropped. But he's not there.

"I'll text him," Jay says, putting the burritos down. "But this is super annoying. I'm hungry. And cold Taco Bell kind of sucks."

We all wait to hear Jay's phone gong and fill the air with the sound of crashing waves as Noah texts back. But nothing comes. I pull out my cell and call. It goes to straight to voicemail.

I'm hungry, too, but now we're all a little concerned. None of us need to say anything; we all have the same idea: *Find Noah now.* We skip the food and search the school. I make Jay search the auditorium while Kate and I take the grounds. We look by the pine tree, by the side entrances, and even around back by the statue of our school mascot—a bronzed Woodhull High Bee whose wings have been defaced with about a million wads of dried, chewed gum.

Jay comes out of the gym, shaking his head. He doesn't look annoyed anymore. He looks nervous.

And I can feel it. Noah is gone. Totally and completely *gone.*

Chapter 6

The Family Rule

There are probably at least fifty gray Honda Civics that cruise through Brecksville, Ohio on any given day. But there's only one that's plastered with NASA mission stickers. And that's Noah Digman's.

Jay, Kate, and I drive around town in the Wagon, craning our necks as we look for Noah's NASA sedan. We check his typical hangouts: the camera store that sells telescopes, Game Stop, even Taco Bell to see if he's circled back to get those burritos. But we have no luck. And at this point, we've each texted him about 14,000 times. No response.

"Okay, before any of us get panicky, let's think," Kate says. But she already sounds panicky. "Where the hell would he go? Is there some science convention he forgot about?"

"Maybe he went to the library," I say. "Like, the *real* library, in town." It wouldn't be the first time he's run off to find a book, just to make sure that something he'd read on the web wasn't complete crap. One of the things I love about Noah is that he loves proving know-it-alls wrong, especially Internet know-it-alls.

"But why wouldn't he answer our texts?" Jay asks, cranking the AC. "Or tell us that he was taking off? He knew we were coming back with the food . . ."

"And it's not like him to miss Taco Bell. For *any* reason." Kate stretches out in the backseat. She fills the car with sounds of loud gum chewing.

"Wait, wait, wait." Jay sits up straight in the passenger seat. I take him literally and slow down. "No, keep driving. Go to my house. He knows where we hide a key."

He does? Why don't I know about this?

I don't get to ask about it because Kate leans into the front seat, blowing and then popping an enormous bubble. "Why would he go to *your* house? You *never* have food at your house."

"Maybe he went to get the cross," Jay says, his voice shaking. "Because he was so freaked out that we'd decide to get rid of it. He didn't want us to get our hands on it."

Now I feel vaguely sick. "And the whole food-run thing was to get rid of us so he could go pick it up . . ."

Kate stops chomping. The car is silent.

WE'RE RIGHT, OF COURSE. I knew we would be. We all knew.

The three of us stand in a semi-circle in Jay's living room, collectively willing Jay's father's prized artifact to return. Willing Noah to return. But the house is empty, and there's nothing on the little table but an outline in the dust where the glass case used to be.

Without a word, we drive straight to Noah's house, but no one answers the doorbell. And none of us know where they might hide a key. We don't see his Honda parked outside, but it could be in the garage. So we go around to the side and look up at his second-story bedroom window. We can't see into his room; the blinds are pulled.

"He's obviously not here," Kate says. "Let's just go. Let's check the library."

Jay ignores her and starts throwing rocks at Noah's window. They ricochet off the glass, getting louder and louder as Jay throws each one harder than the last.

"Dude," I say. "Slow down. You're going to break it."

"He stole something from my house," Jay says, his jaw clenched. "Something important. It belonged to my dad. He deserves a broken window."

"Oh, I love how you're mad now," Kate says with a teasing smile, plopping down in the grass. I know she's trying to soothe him, lighten the mood. Maybe she's as worried as I am that Jay's on the brink of exploding. Behind all of his mellowness there lurks something dark and angry, but then, we all share that to some degree—even Noah. Grief and darkness: they're kind of a package deal. "Just an hour ago you were ready to dump the damn thing in the river."

But Jay keeps throwing rocks. After three more stones, I'm about to rule this useless and head back to the car when something happens: Noah's blinds move. Just a little. But they totally move.

"Did you see that?" Jay asks. His face is still twisted, but his brown eyes sparkle. "I *knew* he was hiding in there. Come on, I think I can guess the garage code. And we can get into the house that way."

We head around front quickly, and Jay starts punching codes into the keypad. But the garage door doesn't budge. The buttons flash alarm-green, and I'm hoping this isn't linked to a security system or something. Like where our fifth incorrect guess at the code will send an alert to the cops and they'll show up, sirens blaring.

"Do you actually have any idea what the code is?" Kate asks, leaning up against the house. "Or are these totally random guesses?"

"I was here when they set it up," Jay mutters, still punching away. "His parents let him pick the number. He never said what it was, but he said something like he wanted it to be a constant so he'd never forget it. I mean, how many constants are in his life? His Honda's model year? His birthdate? The date he first got laid? Wait. That would be never. Maybe four zeroes?"

"He said it was a constant?" I ask, rolling my eyes at Jay's cheap shot. "It's Noah we're talking about. I bet he meant a *mathematical* constant."

Jay smirks. "Um, if I knew what that was, I might be able to wager a guess."

"I bet it's pi," I say. "He loves thinking about Cantor's proof. Move over."

Jay looks confused, but steps aside.

"Cantor's proof?" Kate asks. "A: How and why do you know what that is? And B: Given the fact that you know something like that, why are you failing math?"

"It's about irrational numbers. Like pi. How they're uncountable. Which really messes with your head when you think about it. Plus, pi is a constant," I say, punching it into the keypad. "And I'm failing math because you don't have to care to understand it, but you *do* have to care in order to do things like complete the homework. Or stay awake during the tests."

After I punch in 314, I hit enter. But the garage door doesn't budge.

"Garage codes are usually four numbers," Jay says. "Not three."

"Then somebody Google pi, and give me three decimal places."

Kate jumps on it, swiping and jabbing at her phone. "It's 3.141," she announces, looking up. "And if that works, I am confident that this is the dorkiest garage code in all of Ohio. And perhaps the world."

WE BARREL INTO THE house and head straight for Noah's room. Jay swings the bedroom door open. It's a mess. Like, a total and complete *disaster* area. This is troubling; Noah is the neatest, most methodical guy we know. Anal. He even keeps his pens organized by ballpoint size. His desk, usually organized and super clean, is covered with dusty books and piles of papers. There are several half-full coffee mugs by his green reading lamp.

And sitting in the middle of the desk is his white cat, Sophie. She stands up and purrs, her long tail bumping Noah's blinds.

"Guess that's who we saw in the window," Kate says. She walks over to scratch Sophie behind the ears. Then she peers into one of the coffee cups. "And OMG. There are like, floating spores in there."

Jay picks up a few of the papers that are strewn all over the floor, and Kate goes right for Noah's shelves.

"You guys," I say. "Should we really be going through his stuff like this?"

"We're not friends," Kate says. "We're *family*. And there's a family rule: if we're worried about you, we get to go through your stuff. Besides, *he* felt comfortable enough to go through Jay's stuff and take something that wasn't his, right?"

I shrug and accept this, even though Kate has just proved that the Family Rule is morally dubious. I scan the spines of the books that are piled on the desk. There are titles like *Famous Catholic Mystics* and *The Truth about the Counter-Reformation.* There's one with a map of Rome on the front titled, *First Jesuit Pope: The Francis Effect.* There are books about Spain, orders of priests, religious relics, purgatory, and Catholic teachings about angels and demons. There's one book called *The Afterlife: Visions Shared Across Faiths.* This makes no sense. Of all of us, Noah is the least religious, the least spiritual. He's not into this type of stuff. The nausea I'd felt back in the car returns. My hunger is long forgotten.

"These are my dad's," Jay says, as if reading my mind. He's flipping through the papers on Noah's floor. "I mean, these are the articles he published about his research. And some of his sketches and notes." He gets quiet for a minute. "Noah took these from our house," he says slowly. "These drawings were in a box in my dad's closet."

He holds up a sketch: a drawing of the cross necklace. And the word that is scratched onto the cross is written over and over again in the margins: *magis.*

I stare back at him. Jay's eyes suddenly look empty and sad, like he can't believe his best friend would take this stuff, like he's hoping he's wrong and Kate and I will be able to offer some alternative explanation. We can't.

Instead, I pick up another book and read the title out loud. "*Saint Ignatius of Loyola: The Mysterious Father of the Jesuits.*" I sigh. "He's not reading this because he's Catholic. He isn't really *anything*. And if he *had* to pick a religion, he said it would be Buddhism."

"What the hell?" Jay whispers. "Why does he have all this? We *just* told him about wearing the cross—"

"Today," I say. "We told him today. But look around. He didn't run out and start looking into this in the past hour. Remember how he said the word 'research' right before we left? That's exactly what he's been doing. For a long time."

Jay doesn't respond. Surveying the room again, he takes a deep breath and runs a hand through his thick brown hair.

"I don't like this, you guys," Kate says. She looks pale. "I mean, it's really, really freaky. Why was he researching this? Before he even knew what happened?"

Ignoring my guilt, I decide to embrace Kate's Family Rule and start to rummage through the desk and drawers. The first drawers I try don't help at all; they're just full of school stuff. I slide out the bottom drawer. It's filled with papers and folders and scraps. But they don't look like they're related to homework. I pick up a handful of notes and start to read.

As soon as my eyes focus on the words and my mind puts them together, I let them fall out of my hands. They flutter onto the floor around me like skinny, underfed birds. I grab another handful of papers and read. And then another. And another. *Oh my God.* Now the nausea threatens to make me physically ill. I'd been hoping for clues about where Noah might have gone, where he might want to take the cross. But that's not what I find. The notes are all about the people we've lost—my mom, Kate's aunt, Jay's dad. I find pictures of my mom and notes about things I've said about her. My hands shake as I clutch the papers, my eyes wide at my own handwriting. He's stolen things from me, too. A list I kept in my desk drawer of my mom's favorite things, like humming-birds and irises. There are funny quotes from Kate about her aunt Lilly and her obit from our local paper.

But he's collected the most—and written the most himself— about Jay's dad. There's a timeline of his research, his discoveries. There are lists of people he worked with and a list of Jesuit universities. And he's printed out at least thirty Internet articles about his work.

"Oh, this isn't good," Kate says.

She's grabbed a journal from one of the bookshelves. There's a Black Sabbath bumper sticker on the cover. I recognize it; Noah always claimed it was a math notebook. She opens it and starts reading some of the entries out loud. My ears are buzzing; none of them are about math. Most are about suicide and the afterlife. And every one is dark. "Listen," Kate mutters. "This is his last entry: 'The dark season of fall is cursed. I can't breathe when the leaves start to change. The whole season should be erased because it's the season of rejection.'" She looks up from the pages. Her hands are trembling, too.

"Noah? Suicidal?" Jay asks of nobody in particular. The anger has evaporated. "I don't get it. It's like I don't know him. At all. How could I not know him?"

"And why is fall a time of rejection?" Kate asks. "We haven't even started applying to college yet. Do you think he applied a year early or something? I mean, man cannot get into college on decent science grades alone."

"Hold up," I say. "Let me see that." I take the notebook and heave a sigh of relief. This isn't Noah's handwriting. It's too erratic, too unhinged. "I don't think Noah wrote this," I say, flipping to the front. "Here, look. It says Cam Digman. It was his brother's." I keep searching through the journal, and I spot Noah's writing in the margins. He's taken notes about his brother's entries. Especially the ones Cam made right before he committed suicide. Noah has circled things—like movies Cam watched or things he ate, books he read.

"And check this out," Jay says, moving to Noah's bed. On the wall is a laminated map with pins stuck in it. "Look, it's Catoctin State Park. In Maryland. Where my dad found the cross necklace. It's near a Jesuit retreat center."

Kate flops down on Noah's bed and puts her hands over her face. "This is all so awful. Just awful."

I clutch the journal, trying to stay calm. "What are you thinking?" I ask Jay.

"Maybe he's on his way to put the cross back where my dad found it. It was in a cave somewhere in Catoctin." Jay hesitates, chewing his lip. "Maybe it's like *Indiana Jones and the Last Crusade*. Remember when they tried to take the Holy Grail out of the cave? The German chick who was a spy fell into a chasm, another guy turned to dust, and the whole mountain started to collapse. It was a real spiritual shit storm. It's like a rule or something. Creepy religious artifacts—*you have to put them back*. Maybe Noah figured that's where it belongs, to appease the spirit world or something."

Kate takes her hands away from her face and sits up. "We're talking about Noah. That was a *movie*. Please don't tell me you want to—"

"Jay's right," I say, cutting her off. "If we don't hear from Noah by midnight, then we leave in the morning."

Chapter 7

Help Me.

An uncomfortable truth about my friends: the more they want something, the better they are at lying to get it. Somehow, all three of us convince our parents that we're going to hang out at Noah's for a group study session the whole next day and probably late into the night. And one by one, they all buy it. We can only hope Noah's parents don't call any of *our* parents to ask where the hell he is. But knowing Noah, my guess is that he's texting home with an airtight alibi.

Of course the reality is that we're going to Maryland in my car.

In *theory* it should be fun. Because road trips are supposed to be fun. Once, Kate and I drove the Dragon Wagon all the way to the Hocking Hills just to get our picture with this ginormous wooden Paul Bunyan sculpture. I mean, we *had* to go. How can you *not* go pay homage to a guy whose Wiki page calls him a *lumberjack of unusual skill*? Plus, it gave us a semicultural reason to give our parents for why they should let us drive off into the Ohio sunset with no adult in the car. We didn't even have to lie, really. It worked. And it was awesome.

But a road trip to the hills of Maryland to look for one of your best friends who has taken off with a potentially cursed Catholic cross? Distinctly less awesome.

Kate keeps flipping between country music stations despite group protest. I hear lyrics about red solo cups and wearing lampshades on your head. Jay is in the backseat and opts for headphones.

"Google Maps says this should take almost five hours," I announce as we pull onto the highway. "I'm going to have to demand musical variety."

"What?" Jay leans into the front seat and lifts up his headphones.

"Five hours," I say again. "Too long for a country music marathon."

"We can make it in four-and-a-half if we go about ten miles over the speed limit the whole way. But we all know you like to drive about ten miles *below* the speed limit," he says, nudging me in the shoulder. "You know, because it's good to be prepared for old age."

"Whatever," I say. "We'll be there by two-ish. Home by ten-ish. Our excuse that we're group-studying should hold."

"Group-studying," Kate huffs. "My mom totally knows something is up. But the good news is that I've been around long enough to annoy her to the point of fatigue. She doesn't have any fight left."

Just as I reach up to plug my iPod into the car, a blue station wagon cuts in front of me on the highway. A woman is driving. I can see the outline of her bobbed hair; I think she's wearing a sweater. I drop the iPod cord and speed up, my heart pounding as I pull into the left lane beside her. I can't help but look; I can't help but check to see if it's my mom. But just as I pull close enough to see who is behind the wheel, the woman's car slows way down.

Is this going to torture me for the rest of my life? Searching, always searching?

"Look out!" Kate shouts. I look straight ahead and realize I'm inches away from rear-ending the Range Rover in front of me. I hit the brakes just in time and move back over into the right lane. The woman's car pulls away, and I lose her in traffic.

"Dude," Jay says. "Don't hit a Range Rover."

"Sorry," I say, feeling little beads of sweat on my forehead.

"You sure you're okay to drive?" Kate asks.

"Yeah," I lie.

"Here," she says, plugging my iPod in. "You need to relax. We'll play your music. And roll down the windows. Let's pretend we're just normal sixteen-year-olds having fun on a road trip, shall we?"

So I try. I really do. I tell myself that we'll find Noah safe and sound, that this will all be explained somehow. I roll the windows down as Kate blasts my iPod through the car speakers as loud as it can go. I bob my head for a few beats of "Little Talks." It was my favorite song the year after my mom died. I sing along for a verse or two as the wind blasts through the car. I steal glances at the silver hummingbird charm that hangs from my rearview mirror, as it sways back and forth. It belonged to my mother, and she was never without it. I wanted to bury her with it, but Dad insisted that I keep it. Even though it makes me sad every time it catches the sunlight, every time it sways after I brake at a stop sign, I can't take it down. I just can't.

My mother had a thing with birds. But after she had me, she couldn't see well enough to watch them fly anymore; they were too small in the sky. But she could sit on our back porch near the hummingbird feeder and hear the gentle buzz of their wings as they hovered close. She loved that sound. She called them "my birds," the ones that were made just for her, to make up for all the ones she could no longer see in flight. She said they made it all right, that she didn't miss seeing them play in the wind. She said that she'd accepted not being able to see, that she'd accepted what she'd lost.

But I know it wasn't true. I don't know that it's ever true about loss—real loss, anyway. My deepest, darkest fear is that maybe we don't ever get over some things. Maybe we just carry them around, permanently, these heavy, dull aches in the heart. And maybe they don't heal; maybe we just learn to work around the pain.

I stop singing, shut the iPod off, and put the windows back up. I slow down, make sure I'm driving the speed limit. I know better than to try to enjoy the ride, to try to forget what's happening to us, to forget that having me is what ruined my mother's entire existence. Joyrides won't ever feel right. Ever.

"Sorry," I say, as soon as the all the windows are back up. "Can't really get into the whole road trip thing right now. And can somebody try Noah again?"

"I texted him about two minutes ago," Kate says. "He's still incommunicado."

I think about Noah in his fake periodic table T-shirt with his sparkling blue eyes and his tell-me-everything look. He feels like a stranger now, and I hate it. None of this is like him, to disappear like this, to keep things from us. We *do* have a Family Rule: we tell each other everything. *Everything*. The good, the bad, the dark, the scary. And especially the stuff that has anything to do with the people we've lost, the deaths we've all been marked by. And I realize I'm mad at him, but more than that—I'm worried. Because I know if he's keeping secrets, it must be for a reason. A really, really good reason. *What did you know about all of this, Noah? What did you know?*

"Can you read the stuff you brought?" I ask, eyeing Jay in the rearview mirror. "From Noah's room?"

"You *sure* you want to try and figure this out right now?" Kate looks at me like a worried parent, or like I'm some sort of delicate plant that might wilt and die at any moment if someone doesn't figure out *exactly* how to take care of me. I nod. "Okay then," she says. "Jay, read us some of the crap you brought from his room. Go."

Jay shuffles through the pile of papers he scooped up from Noah's floor. "I mean, all we know is that the cross belonged to Saint Ignatius and that it's all scratched up and has the word *magis* on it, right?" I ask to speed things along.

"Right," Jay says. "I used to know who he was and all, but it's been a long time. Hang on." He starts skimming an article. "Um, Saint Ignatius of Loyola. This says he was a Spanish knight, a hermit, then a priest, then a saint, *blah, blah, blah.* Religious mystic during the Counter-Reformation, *blah, blah, blah.* Wait. Let me read more and then I'll paraphrase."

We ride in silence as he reads his dad's articles. The absence of sound lasts too long. My fingers drum on the wheel. I start checking cars again for my mom. I imagine her pulling up in a car beside me on the highway, slowly looking over. I imagine her smile. But then her face changes, like she's afraid, that she sees or knows something horrifying that she wants me to know, but can't tell me. And then I imagine her disappearing again.

"Okay," Jay says finally. He leans into the front seat with

an article in his hands. "Here's the upshot: he was born in 1491 and before he became a saint, his real Spanish name was Iñigo de Loyola."

I try to shake off the image of my mom and my worries about Noah and focus on what Jay is saying. "Go on."

"And he lived in the Basque region of Spain and his family was super wealthy," Jay continues. "He was totally vain and obsessed with women, and he was kind of a slacker—he didn't even know Latin all that well. He was in love with the sister of Emperor Charles the Fifth. And he always wore the latest fashions—like men's tights and a codpiece."

"Ooh," Kate says, holding up her phone. "I'm Googling *codpiece*. Sounds like fishing gear. But maybe it's super sexy, like tights."

I laugh in spite of myself. I have the urge to reach over and hug Kate. Jay ignores her and keeps going. "And in 1521, his leg was practically blown off by a cannonball in a battle with the French. While he was recovering, he ran out of books to read. So he picked up a book about the saints. And he felt inspired and thought he had a vision of an angel or something."

"Found it," Kate says, "Codpiece. Popular in the fifteenth and sixteenth centuries. A sack that attaches to men's pants and accentuates and holds their . . ." She giggles. "Yup. I was right."

"About what?" I ask.

"Let's just say that you use a codpiece to fish—*for the ladies.*"

"Forget about what he wore," Jay grumbles. "Anyway, he ditched the codpiece. Listen; this is important. So after Ignatius saw some sort of angel, he completely freaked out, left the rich life behind, and started praying in a cave seven hours a day in a little Spanish town called Manresa. He let his hair grow, started dressing in rags. People thought he was a lunatic. They had a nickname for him—El Hombre Saco, which meant Old Sack Man."

I nod, trying not to look over at Kate in case she'll make me laugh. And even though laughing can make that dull ache go away, even for just a moment, Jay's right; this is important. Noah is missing. I can't lose another person I love. I pull the sun visor down to keep the glare out of my eyes. "Okay. Let's review. So a wealthy Spanish guy gets hit by a cannonball, freaks out, sees an angel, renounces his old life, and goes to live in a cave . . ."

"Right, and this is where it gets interesting," Jay says. He leans back, skimming and flipping through pages. "So after praying in the cave for about a million hours, he had some sort of crazy enlightenment-flash-of-white-light moment by the Cardoner River. His cross necklace got so hot it burned his skin, and he said he could write for the rest of his life and not communicate all that he learned in that one instant. So he went back into the cave and tried to write down as much as he could in a book he called *The Spiritual Exercises*. It became one of the most famous theology books of all time. All it says here is that it gives directions about how to make good decisions in life and talks about how everyone should get quiet and practice *spiritual discernment*. Whatever that is. The end."

I shoot him a quick smile in the rearview. "Nice paraphrasing," I say. "Thanks."

"And I Googled *magis*," Kate says, her voice serious now, too. "It's Latin. For more."

"So let's review again," I say, my mind reeling with Jay's history lecture. "This guy etched the word *more* on the back of the cross necklace he had on during his epiphany—which is the cross we all wore," I say. "And he had some sort of revelation about how to make decisions? And wrote a famous book about it. And as far as Noah goes, that helps us understand . . . exactly nothing."

Jay sighs. "I know, I know. But Saint Ignatius is pretty famous I guess—if you're a Catholic. It says his book became the foundation for the Jesuits. You know, they started a bunch of universities and they're all into social justice and stuff. And Noah has written a note on the side. *Pope Francis, elected March 13, first Jesuit pope in history.*"

I shake my head, staring at the highway. I'm more confused then ever. "How the hell did your dad find the necklace in the first place?" I wonder out loud. "I mean, the guy was Spanish. It was around the time of Columbus. Hardly any Europeans were here. The necklace was in a cave in *Maryland.*"

Kate shifts in her seat and sighs loudly. "First, it's not all *that* surprising. Think about it—MARY-land. The whole state was like, founded by Catholics, for Catholics. His cross must have been sent here to his Jesuit buddies for good luck in the New World or something."

I nearly gasp. I know that Jay shares the silent shock that reverberates through the car. To say that Kate would be the *last human on earth* we would expect to know any United States history would be an understatement so huge it would be virtually immeasurable. But the smirk Jay and I share in the rearview also sends a pang through me. Noah should be here, to share in this moment, too. He'd practically faint if he heard Kate spewing facts about US states.

"What's the second point?" Jay asks.

"That if I'm going to be called upon to absorb any more of this theology presentation, I'm going to need a Diet

Mountain Dew." Kate runs a hand over her forehead like she's already mentally exhausted. "Scratch that. I need a full-sugar Dew. And chewy Sweet Tarts."

I TAKE AN EXIT near Newton Falls.

"Who names a gas station Sheetz?" Kate says as I ease into a spot by a pump. "It sounds like they sell gas, snacks, and a room for a quickie in the back."

"There's a Speedway four miles from here. Gas is two cents cheaper per gallon," Jay says, urgently tapping my shoulder from the backseat.

"How do you know that?" I say.

"Gas price app," he says, waving his phone. "It's the bomb."

I resist the urge to tell him he sounds as dorky as Noah right now. I don't want to think about Noah until I can scream at him face-to-face for all he's done.

"Yeah, but do you have an app that tells you whether the Speedway has a slushie machine?" Kate asks, flipping her long black hair over her shoulder. "Because I can see one inside the Sheetz, and I *need* a slushie. And some gummy worms."

"I thought you needed Sweet Tarts and a Dew?" Jay asks. He stows his papers and books in the way-back, maybe mentally exhausted himself.

"I'm wildly unpredictable like that," Kate says dryly, hopping out.

I head for the pump, but Jay beats me there.

"I'll do it." His fingers brush mine as we both reach for the pump handle.

"Dude," I say, raising an eyebrow. "Thanks, but this isn't a guys-pump-gas-while-girls-go-to-the-bathroom thing is it? Because I can totally pump my own—"

"Hold on, Susan B. Anthony," he says with a smile. "You're driving and all, and I just thought I could do something nice. Go in. Have a slushie. Relax."

Again, I wish Noah were here, so we could finish our last conversation, so I could say to him: *See, this is why I'm into Jay. He really is wildly unpredictable. And always in the best way and always at the right time.*

But then I imagine the super intense eye roll Noah would give me if I actually proclaimed this about Jay. And how he'd probably nail me for labeling someone who plays a loop of exactly three Pink Floyd songs and likes the same parade of popular girls *wildly unpredictable*. I shake it off and follow Kate into Sheetz.

She immediately heads for the slushie machine, filling a cup the size of her head with bright red frozen goo. I look around at all my options—Fritos, nuts, granola bars, candy, gum, pop, fifteen million types of water. Thoughts I don't want to have start swirling in my head. I think about my mom, the flapper girl in the auditorium, Jay's dad. I look around at the other shoppers, my eyes locking on each one to see if any of them look old-fashioned or out of place. Suddenly, I can't handle being in here. All the strangers start to look sinister to me and the fluorescent lights remind me too much of the grocery store where I saw Mom. I hit the door a little too hard on my way out and the bell above it jangles madly as I head toward the parking lot.

And that's when I hear my name. It's a raspy whisper. Frantic almost. Coming from—

"Riley."

I hear it again. I follow the sound around to the left, behind the building. There, sitting on the asphalt, leaning up against a huge dumpster, is a woman who looks homeless. Her face is smeared with grime, and her hair is a tangled brown mess. A bottle of booze peeks out from the ratty handbag she's holding. She takes a long swig and smiles. We lock eyes, and then, like a flickering light, I see another woman in her place.

Instead of a mad nest of hair, this new woman I see has a long, neat braid hanging over her shoulder, and she's wearing a veil and a white old-fashioned dress—a wedding dress with puffy sleeves and antique, yellowed lace. Her dainty feet are suddenly laced up in white leather boots. And she says something to me. And I hear it, and I understand it, but it's terrifying, and immediately I try to push it out of my mind.

As I back away, she changes again—back to the homeless woman in dirty clothes and ripped jeans, swigging booze from a beaten-up handbag.

I want to run, to scream, but it's like one of those dreams where you're being chased but you can't get away or make a sound louder than a whisper. I back away from the dumpster as quickly as I can, but I feel like I'm moving through waist-high peanut butter—my legs feel thick and heavy, and as usual, a wave of numbness starts crashing over me. I turn and walk to the car in a half-daze, climb into the back seat, and slam the door shut.

"Whoa, you okay?" Jay asks, opening the door.

"Yep," I say, staring straight ahead at nothing.

"Okay, you *said* yes, but it's obviously a no."

I just keep staring into space; I keep thinking about that wedding dress, hearing the bride's raspy voice.

Kate comes back, her arms loaded down with drinks, snacks, and a giant slushie. "Why are you in the backseat?" she asks me. "Oh, god. You look awful. What happened?" She holds out a Vitamin Water for me, but I wave it away. "Did you see someone?"

I nod.

"Your mom?"

I shake my head no. "A homeless woman," I say. My voice is so calm, so flat, that it scares me. "By the dumpster. She turned into some old-timey bride. In a wedding dress." My throat catches, and I stop. "But this time it was different."

"Different how?" Jay asks.

"She said something to me."

"OMG," Kate says. "OMG. What did she say?"

The numbness cracks for just a second, and I feel the closest I've come to crying since the day I buried my mom. But of course I don't. I just shove it down to that place deep inside, to the vast emotional graveyard where all feelings other than "fine" go to die.

"Help me," I quote.

"We *will*," Kate says, grabbing my hand. "I'm seeing things, too. We're in this together. We're here for you—"

"No," I say. "That's what the bride said. *Riley. Help me.*"

Chapter 8

Little Voices

We're quiet the rest of the way. Jay drives because I'm in no shape to be behind the wheel. I stretch out in the backseat and try to rest. Except I don't. At all. Every time I close my eyes, all I see is that bride by the dumpster; I hear her voice over and over.

I text Noah again. I ask where he is. I ask him to text me something, anything—a comma, a period, any emoji he wants—just to let me know he's okay.

But he doesn't text back.

About three and a half hours in, we start seeing signs for tourists, advertisements for things to do in Maryland. I try to read every sign to keep my mind in the present, to slow my brain down. There's a billboard for a restaurant called Medieval Meals where for fifty dollars you can get all the large turkey legs and jousting you can handle—all inside a "real castle." The only problem is that you can tell from the picture that the "real castle" is totally and obviously made of cinderblocks. Then there's a sign for Assateague Island where apparently a large herd of ponies "still runs free" and you can "bond with the horse spirit."

It's a testament to how scared we are that no one comments on any of this. Dinner and fake jousting in a cinderblock castle? A pony island with "ass" as its root word? But even Kate can't muster a wisecrack.

IT'S JUST BEFORE TWO o'clock when we reach Catoctin Mountain Park. Kate holds the map we took down from Noah's wall and calls out directions as we take a winding road that curves through the entrance. It feels darker than it should at this time of day; the sunlight is muted by crowded pine trees and oaks. Jay drives up a steep hill past a small, muddy lake. Ducks waddle underneath a sign that reads in chipped-off paint: RIDENHOUR LAKE. We drive for what feels like ages and finally come to the southern border of the park. Kate tells Jay to stop.

"There was a pin on the map here," she says. "And a line down this road and up a creek."

"But this will take us just outside the park," Jay says.

"I know, but look," Kate points at the map. "This is where Noah's pin was, and the line goes right down this road."

I sit up to get a closer look. "What's that writing? There? Is it a number?"

"Four twenty-six," Jay says. "No idea what that means."

Jay pulls the car to the side of the road and we all get out and start walking. Intense heat comes off the dark pavement; the smell of baking tar floats up my nose. Dragonflies hover in the humid air, and I swat big black flies away from my arms.

Finally, we reach a driveway with a mailbox. It's 426 Blake's

Creek Road. And at the end of it is a house—a plain white one-story farmhouse that looks normal enough. Next to the driveway is a creek. It snakes through the property and disappears into thick woods beside a pasture where several horses graze and swat at flies with their long stringy tails. A sleek chestnut one stomps a hoof on the ground, sending a shudder over his skin, knocking the flies off all at once.

Jay and I turn to Kate.

"This is the creek," she says, looking at the map again. "But this isn't park property. What if whoever lives here sees us, like, trespassing? I mean, I want to find Noah—but I really don't want to get shot in the process."

"Then stay low as we walk up the creek," Jay instructs her. "The banks will keep us hidden."

"I don't like this," she says. "I need someone to hold my hand."

So Jay grabs Kate's hand and we make our way down into the creek, the shallow water churning a muddy brown beneath us. I don't like this, either, but I know we have no other choice. After creeping quietly along for maybe twenty minutes, I start to get nervous. What if we get lost? What if we're not really in the right place like Kate thinks? The banks get higher and higher the farther we go. Massive slabs of rock jut out of the earth; green moss and lichens crawl over damp surfaces. A few small waterfalls pour between boulders; some trees have initials carved into their sides. We come to a fork in the creek and pause while Jay and Kate study the map. Jay is sweating a little and seems edgy, like when we were in the cemetery together.

"I don't see a fork on the map," he says, peering over Kate's shoulder.

Kate blinks at the map. "Maybe this is the wrong creek?"

"Let me see that," I say, taking it from her. But I can't make any more sense of it than she can.

"Let's go right," Kate says. "No. Left. My first idea is always the wrong one."

Often your second, too. But we keep going, to the left. I hear a snapping branch and turn. I scan the woods around us, but all I see are endless trees, their trunks like soldiers standing guard.

"Did you hear something?" Kate asks.

"Yeah," I say. "Like a snapping twig or something? Or—"

"Voices," Kate says, stiffening. "I hear voices."

"Wait. I hear them, too," Jay says. He narrows his eyes. "I hear kids."

And then I hear them, as well. They get louder as we continue up the creek. I hear what sounds like a small boy shouting and then a girl answering back. We pick up our pace. For some reason, we all seem to forget that we're trespassing.

"Noah?" I call. I do it again. My cry echoes through the creek bed. I wonder if Kate and Jay are thinking what I am . . . that these voices don't sound quite right; they sound processed in some way. Like they seem to be all around us, but at the same time, they sound distant. And distressed.

"Let's just go back," Kate says, stopping mid-creek. "Seriously."

But Jay walks ahead, listening. Ever since I've known him, he's had a thing about kids in trouble. He's always looking out for them. If he sees one fall on a playground, he rushes to help. If we're watching a movie and a kid is about to get hurt, he turns it off. He can't stand to see kids in pain. He wants the world to abide by some unbreakable rule that children are not allowed to be harmed. That they should be protected from witnessing horrible things, especially the things that adults can't explain or give good reasons for. Like why someone can't stop drinking and has to fall down the basement stairs and die.

"Jay, come on," Kate protests. "Let's just go." I can tell she's about to fall apart. She's looking all around us, up and down the creek and even into the trees, searching for the voices. Her hands are trembling.

But Jay keeps moving, fast.

"Noah?" he calls into the woods. My heart thumps. I grab Kate's hand. I want to leave, run down this creek and never look back. I can hear the voices in my bones, like the children have crawled inside my body and are screaming from the inside out.

"Dammit," Kate says. "There he goes."

I spot the small cave ahead just as Jay vanishes inside it. Squeezing each other's hands more tightly, Kate and I approach the mouth and squint into the blackness.

"Come on!" he calls to us from a place I can't see.

Now I can hear what sounds like teenagers laughing—or are they crying?

Kate abruptly lets go of me and starts backing down the creek.

"What are you doing?" I ask. She just shakes her head. "Kate. Come on. We go after him. And maybe Noah is in there. Maybe he's in trouble. We go in. *Obviously.*"

I don't have to explain the *obviously*. Kate knows better. We clean up the puke after games of Truth of Dare; we sit under willow trees and chew mounds of gum; we tell each other the lie that *it'll be okay*. That's all we want for each other. That's all we want for Noah at this moment. *Obviously* we go in the cave.

"Okay, okay," Kate says, sighing. "Sorry. My bad. Hold my hand again?"

I roll my eyes. *Obviously.*

THE AFTERNOON SUN QUICKLY disappears behind us and the air goes cool and quiet as we make our way into the cave. The tunnel angles down, and I follow it deeper and deeper, leading Kate as gently as I can. I'm suddenly aware of the weight of the earth above me, and it makes me feel pretty close to helpless. If this cave wants to crush me, it can. If it wants to flood, unannounced, and bury me in a watery grave, it can. I read once that when you take tours through caves, you're never supposed to touch the walls. The oil from the fingertips of tourists damages the cave ecosystem. Mineral rock deposits that have been forming into long and beautiful stalagmites and stalactites are stopped by our touch. The delicate balance of moisture and temperature is disturbed. The idea that the cave needs to be protected from me is comforting. I like not being the only vulnerable one.

Kate taps on her iPhone light and clings to my side. I call for Jay and then for Noah, my voice echoing against the cave walls. We wait and listen for an answer back.

Silence.

But then the voices start again, like wisps of smoke I can smell but can't see. And again, they seem to be coming from all directions at once.

"I'm freaking out," Kate says. "Sing something. Anything."

"Like what?"

"Something happy. From childhood. Like a nursery rhyme."

"Fine," I say, too freaked out to protest. *"Mary had a little lamb,"* I begin weakly, my voice cracking. But then I take a deep breath and find the right notes. *"Whose fleece was white as snow—"*

"Whoa," Kate says. She stops and shines the light right at me. "You do know that your voice is, like, beautiful or something. We need to get you on a stage somewhere."

"Shut up," I say, bending down to avoid a low hanging rock. "I'll sing in the car with you guys. But that's it. No stages."

"Why not?"

I glance over my shoulder at her. "I don't sing in front of people. I just—don't. No real reason."

Even in the dim iPhone light, I can see the face Kate makes. *Obviously* there's a reason. And now, thanks to my best friend, in the unrelenting blackness of the cave, that reason flashes in my mind, bright and depressing as an aisle of grocery store fluorescents.

WHEN I WAS ELEVEN I figured out I could sing. Like, *really* sing. I came in from playing outside and saw my mother in the living room, sitting on the couch with an electronic keyboard in her lap. And it had this little stand sticking up in the back that held a piece of sheet music. Mom was hunched over, squinting at it, her face all scrunched up and only inches from the page. I knew she couldn't see well enough to read a sheet of music, and I didn't understand why she was even trying. One wrong note after the other filled the air. She'd hit a key that didn't go with the last and sigh—a deep, this-is-about-way-more-than-a-song sigh—lots of them.

"Where'd you get the keyboard?" I asked.

"Your father bought it for me," she said, still squinting at the sheet music. "We went to Gordy's, that little music store downtown? And they didn't have my favorite sheet music in braille. It's so frustrating. But your father thought I should try playing again."

I hopped onto the couch next to her, sidling close. My feet didn't quite touch the ground. I remember looking down at my black Converse sneakers swinging just above the carpet. Those were the only shoes I would agree to wear until I was twelve years old. Even when I was forced to wear a Christmas dress, and then an Easter dress, and then a dress for the stupid sixth grade dance—I wore them all with black Chucks.

"He thought you should try again?" I asked.

"Well, I used to play," she said absently. "We used to have a real piano. Sat over there in that corner. But that was before . . ."

She didn't have to finish the sentence, because I could guess what the rest of it was. *Before.* Before I came along, before the stroke during childbirth wrecked her eyesight, before her life was completely messed up by yours truly. A lump formed in the back of my throat, so tight it was almost painful. I remember thinking that sadness felt like getting sick—like strep throat or a cold or the flu.

I knew she couldn't see my face, but she must have sensed what I was feeling. "I used to do the Hula-Hoop, too," she joked. "Some things you just outgrow."

But I knew she hadn't outgrown the piano. She'd *lost* it. So I tried, in my eleven-year-old way, to fix the situation.

"What if we sing?" I asked. "You don't have to see sheet music to sing a song you know."

"No, no," Mom said, tucking a strand of her chestnut hair behind her ear. "I'm a terrible singer. But you sing. That would be lovely to hear you."

So I stood up, right in the middle of the living room, and

tried to think of a song. I opted for the very first one I ever learned: "Twinkle, Twinkle, Little Star." I wanted to make her happy with my voice, so I put everything I had into my little performance. I threw in a few runs here and there and kind of spiced it up a little. And I could tell by my mom's face that she was into it. Like, *really* into it.

"Riley," she said slowly. "Your voice is gorgeous. How did I not know you could sing like that? Sing it again."

And so I did. And at first, she looked so happy. But then there was something else. Something about the way she was looking at me as I continued to belt out the notes. It wasn't pure joy; it wasn't plain happiness at seeing her daughter spread her wings and find a talent. There was wistfulness, an I'm-happy-for-you-but-sad-for-me quality in her half-smile. And when I finished the song, it didn't feel good anymore. It felt bad, slightly wrong, like my talent and my life were the consolation prizes my mother received for losing her own.

That was the moment I decided that I shouldn't sing in front of people. Or ever try to do the Hula-Hoop.

KATE TURNS HER IPHONE light away from me and sighs. "Well, I guess I should feel relieved that I'm not the only one who hasn't shared *everything*. You'll tell me once we're out of here. Deal?"

"Deal," I whisper. "We continue to pick our way through the tunnel and bend down low again as we round a tight corner. But on the other side, the cave abruptly ends.

"What the hell?" Kate says as she flashes her light along the walls and the ceiling. "Where's Jay? Where could he have gone?"

I run my hands along the walls, looking for an exit. And

then I feel it: a tiny opening to our right, barely big enough to crawl through.

"Look," I say. Kate flashes her light on the hole. "You don't think he—?"

"Yeah. I do," she says. "He totally went through there."

Kate's iPhone casts a pale, weak light on our faces, but it's enough to see how worried she looks. The cave could collapse on Jay and kill him instantly; it could collapse on us. Maybe it's already collapsed on Noah. We might never be found. She arches her eyebrows, asking.

"Obviously," I mouth silently.

Kate's shoulders sag, but she shimmies through the hole. I follow her into the narrow passageway; the ceiling is so low we have to get on our stomachs and pull ourselves along. After about ten seconds, I'm out of breath from the crawling, and I start to feel claustrophobic.

Kate's light alone isn't strong enough in this cramped darkness, so I reach for my phone and tap on the flashlight app, hoping a little more light will calm me down. But it doesn't. In the light I can see just how tight a space we're in. There are only a few inches of room between the craggy rock walls and me. I frantically shine the light all around and above—and that's when I see the drawing.

I manage to roll over on my back to get a better look.

Etched deep into the stone is an image of a man in a cloak with rays of light emanating from his head, terrifying and beautiful all at once. He clutches a book in his left hand and dangling from his right hand is a cross necklace. And below it is that word—*magis*.

More.

I want to call out to Kate, tell her about the drawing, tell her we've found it: the place where Jay's dad found the necklace. But suddenly the thick darkness, the voices, the small space—it's too much for me. My lungs lock up, and I push myself back out toward the opening. I try to get a deep breath, but I can't; my chest is too tight. I struggle hard to get out as tiny bits of rock and dust fall from the ceiling. My hands burn as I fight against the rough sides of the tunnel. *I just want out.* But then I hear another voice: Jay's.

"Riley!" He's shouting from the other end of the tunnel. "Kate! You guys okay?"

"Jay?" I manage.

"Are you all stuck?"

"I can't breathe. There's a drawing—" My chest jerks up and down as I fight for an even breath.

"I know," he says. "I saw it. Just keep coming. Come toward my voice, you guys. You're almost there. There's a huge room at this end. Come on."

"We're coming," Kate calls, scrambling ahead of me. "Riley? You got this. Just take it slow. Go towards Jay's voice. Okay?"

I don't say anything back, but I manage to start moving forward again, toward Kate, who has taken it upon herself to pretend that she's suddenly courageous—for my sake. Their voices are like ladders; each word a rung I grip and pull. I close my eyes and ignore the sounds of the children still echoing around me. I think about how Jay looked a few days ago when he showed up at my door, sickly pale and terrified because he'd just seen his dead father. I think about walking through the door to get to him, to lead him up to my room. I think about the feeling of us pressed together on the porch that night with the fireflies blinking like Christmas lights all around us.

And then I feel him. He reaches in and grabs my arm.

As soon as he touches me, I feel like I take the breath that saves my life; I couldn't have survived another second in that tunnel. I put my other hand up toward him, and he takes it and pulls. Hard. He drags me out of the tunnel, and I lie on my back in a large opening. The air is cold and rushes into my lungs. He bends over me and gently wipes the dust from my face.

"Sorry," he says as he puts his arm around me, "that I didn't wait for you guys. I was just so—"

"Oblivious to the fact that you abandoned your two best girl friends in a cave?" The words come out in a jumbled rush.

"Worried about the *kids*," Jay says softly. "And Noah."

I sit up and Jay pulls me to my feet. Kate points her iPhone light all along the cave walls. Jay's right; the cavern is enormous.

"But they're not here," he says. "It dead ends, there's no—" He starts but is cut off by the sound of a child's giggle. I hold my breath and listen.

"Let's just go, then," Kate pleads. "We'll send for help."

"But we're at the end," Jay says. "There are no more openings, and we didn't pass any side tunnels along the way. Where are the voices coming from?"

"Maybe there were passageways we didn't see," I say, to avoid suggesting what I'm certain we're all thinking, that the voices are just the aural versions of what we've seen since discovering the cross. "They could be a mile farther down some side tunnel we missed. Maybe Noah is with them."

"Okay, we'll go. But if Noah was here to put the cross back, then it's probably in this room somewhere," Jay says, sweeping his phone light around the walls. "Let's at least try to find it before we bail."

We each take a wall and run our hands along them, looking for a place where Noah might have hidden the cross: a hole, a break in the rock, a little indentation.

Kate freezes. "I think I found something," she says.

I stop and point my iPhone light at her. She's found another drawing, just like the one in the tunnel. Etched into the cave wall is the small figure of a man holding a cross and a book. And below it, there's a nook that's covered up with tiny stones. We watch as she gently pulls the rocks away and uncovers a small shelf in the cave wall, about the size of a loaf of bread. She slowly reaches in and pulls something out. *Is it the cross?* Suddenly I feel so desperate to see the cross necklace again, as if it will take me directly to my mom, as if it's a piece of her itself. I hold my breath even though my lungs still burn with cave dust.

"Check this out," she says.

My thudding heart sinks. She's holding a very old-looking, very thin book.

And then—silence.

The voices are suddenly quiet, hushed instantly as if someone hit *stop*. The only sound I hear now is a slow drip of water from the cave ceiling. Jay's eyes are as wide as mine. Kate blows the dust off the book's cover and wipes it a few times with her sleeve. We group around her as she holds her iPhone light on its leather cover.

The title is etched in a fancy, looping script, and I can barely make out words:

Gogo-Jardunak

"Whoa," Jay says slowly. "Is that Spanish?"

"No," I say, leaning a little closer over Kate's shoulder. "I may only have a C in that class, but even I know that's not Spanish. Not even close. Except—" I peer at the cover. "But see these words, down here? I think that's *a-r-a-b-e-r-a?* And then, *Iñazio Loiolako.*"

"Iñazio looks like Iñigo," Jay says. "Ignatius's Spanish name before he was a saint. And you think *Loiolako,* is—"

"Yeah," I say. "I think it says Ignatius of Loyola."

"I'm going to pass out," Kate whispers, leaning on me.

"And check it out, inside," Jay says, gently flipping through the pages. "This whole thing is *handwritten.*" He turns to the last page and there, at the very bottom, is the name again, a signature this time: *Iñazio Loiolako, 1522.*

"And what year did he write his famous book?" I ask.

"Fifteen twenty-two," Jay says slowly.

"So are you thinking this is like, his original?" Kate asks.

"Maybe," Jay says. "But if it is, then I'm totally confused. Noah's map led us right to it. And Noah got all of his research from my dad's stuff. If it was so easy to find, why didn't my dad find it? He never found a manuscript, just the cross."

"Exactly," I say. "And if Noah was actually here, hell-bent on putting the cross back, then where is it?"

I look back at the book's dusty cover. I'm not thinking how amazing it is that we might have just discovered a saint's original manuscript, an important historical artifact. I'm thinking about the only thing that really matters—that maybe this book will explain the cross necklace. That maybe this book will tell me why I saw my mom. And more importantly, *maybe it will tell me how to make her come back.*

Chapter 9

Lost in Translation

It's not until we're back in the car and almost completely out of the state park that we have a signal strong enough to Google the manuscript. None of our phones buzz or gong or chime with incoming texts or voicemails from Noah. I begin to wonder if he even went to the cave at all. But we don't have time to second-guess ourselves. It's 4:15 and we have to be back by ten.

Jay drives while Kate and I work our phones. The first hits I get don't say anything about the history of the book itself, but finally, I find some information in an online Catholic dictionary.

"Here," I say. "It says the original version that Saint Ignatius wrote right after his enlightenment is missing and was never published. The only version that was shown to the pope and published in 1548 was a watered-down Latin translation. Apparently, Ignatius was too afraid to reveal the original because the Roman Inquisition was going on. The Jesuits were getting persecuted."

Kate gasps. "So if we're right and we just found the 1522 original—no one has ever read it?"

"Looks like it," Jay says. His voice is faraway, his eyes on the road but cloudy. I can tell he's thinking of his dad, spinning his wheels, wondering why his dad didn't find it if he was right there in that cave. I'm wondering the same thing.

"OMG," Kate says, her eyes lighting up. "We have to figure out what it says. STAT."

My stomach twists into a knot. I agree. I want this book to tell me why I saw my mom; I want it to tell me how to see her again. Even if it's just for one last time.

"Okay," Jay says, slowing to exit. "But I'm going to need food."

A few minutes later, he wheels into the parking lot of a Subway, apparently making the executive decision that ancient book translation calls for a five-dollar foot-long sandwich.

"Driver gets to pick the food," he says as he parks. "We'll be quick."

Kate and I concede, grab the manuscript, and follow him. An electronic bell bing-bongs to announce our arrival.

"Welcome to Subway!" the girl behind the counter chirps. She's wearing a black Subway visor, a skin-tight white tank top, even tighter jeans, and her nametag (Crystal, Sandwich Artist) is stuck on her shirt exactly at nipple level. It clings there like a tiny mountain climber terrified it's going to slip from the perilous slopes of Crystal's breast and plunge into the vat of tuna salad below. "What can I make for you today?"

Except her question doesn't sound normal. It sounds *southern*. Like her words have gotten subdued on their way out of her mouth, slowed to a crawl by some mysterious force that lurks in the Appalachian Mountains and preys on unsuspecting vowels.

Jay stands below the Order Here sign, and stares at Crystal like an animal in heat. *Really?* I think. The silent pause is excruciating as he launches into an open and obvious ogle. I gently nudge him out of my way. "I'll take a six-inch chicken on honey-oat. And he'll take a drool cup. Thanks."

He blushes, but finally manages to squeak out a sandwich order.

When Crystal finishes our subs, we fill our cups at the pop machine, pick out bags of chips, and settle into a booth by the window.

"So does anyone have any great ideas about the fastest way to translate a sixteenth century manuscript that's written in who-knows-what language?" I ask. Kate shakes her head no, but Jay doesn't even respond. He's acting super awkward and is all thumbs with his sandwich. He can't even get the thing out of the bag. "I guess Jay will weigh in when the testosterone fog lifts?"

Kate laughs with her cheeks stuffed full of chips. "Don't tell me you're jealous of the super-stacked sandwich artist . . ."

I reach for the manuscript, but Jay stops me, suddenly waking from his Hot Sub Girl reverie.

"Whoa," he says. "Wipe your hands first. You're about to get sweet onion teriyaki sauce on a priceless religious artifact." He takes the book and starts gently flipping through the pages. "The whole thing is in that *crazy* language. Somebody pull up Google Translate. It has a detect-language feature."

I'm glaring at Jay for being such a jerk, but shove the feeling aside. Besides, this isn't about him; it's about Noah. I'm the quickest draw at the table and have the website pulled up on my phone in like .5 seconds. "Ready," I say.

"Okay, let's start with the title. Put in *Gogo-Jardunak.*"

So I do. I type it in slowly. And the result comes up right away.

"It says Basque detected," I say. "Never heard of it. Anyone else?"

Jay nods. "It's a region of Spain. It's in that stuff in the car, those articles. It's a region in the north, near the Pyrenees Mountains between Spain and France . . ."

"Hold up. Googling," Kate says, tapping her iPhone screen. "Basque. Internet says it's the ancestral language of the Basque people, the only remnant of the language spoken in Southwest Europe before the region was Romanized in the second century. And it's a 'language isolate,' whatever that means."

"But why is it not in Latin?" I ask, looking at Jay. "I mean, it just seems like the ancient European saint thing to do: write in Latin."

"Yeah," Jay says, stuffing his sub in his mouth, muffling his speech. "But the backshtory shaid he washn't a very educated guy at firsht. Didn't know Latin."

"Gross. Can you chew first?" I say. Seeing my opportunity, I grab the manuscript and plug the first three major words from the first page into Google Translate: *sekretuak,* *nire,* and *ilustrazioaren.* The meanings pop up straight away. *Sekretuak* means "secrets" in Basque, *nire* means "my" and *ilustrazioaren* means "illustration."

I look up.

"Need a pen?" Kate asks, reading my mind, per usual. She reaches into her purse and hands me a pen that appears brand new—clearly never used for actual note-taking in class.

I jot the words down on a Subway napkin. "So I think

this first sentence says something about the secrets of his illustration."

"I bet it means more like, enlightenment," Jay says once he's swallowed another huge mouthful. "He's writing about the secrets of his enlightenment. The one he had by the Cardoner River. I don't think Saint Ignatius was an artist."

"But what about the drawings in the cave?" I ask.

Jay shrugs.

I type in the third word into the Basque box—*nuntavatious.* And the English translation is—*nuntavatious.*

"I don't get it," I say, typing it in again. "It's just spitting the word back out at me instead of translating it."

"Let me see," Jay says, taking my phone. "Yep. That's what Google Translate does when it doesn't know the word. It just repeats it in the translation box."

"Maybe it's not Basque," Kate pipes in. "Try language detect again."

And I do. And it detects *nuntavatious* as Finnish. But still doesn't translate the word. I type it in again, and this time it guesses Slovak.

"Guessing Finnish," Kate says. "And Slovak. That's Google Translate's way of saying W-T-F, my friends. W-T-F."

"Shit," I say. "We need a plan. GT isn't going to be able to handle all of these words."

"I have an idea," Kate says.

She hops up and bolts back to the drink station, returning with two enormous handfuls of napkins. She looks at us like we're supposed to get why the hell she has nearly emptied the Subway napkin supply. This time, for once, our mutual mind-reading abilities have failed us completely.

"We're going to need an explanation," Jay says.

"One sec," she says. "I'm just taking a moment to marvel at my organizational genius."

The impromptu-sub-shop-translation strategy is this: First, Jay will scan a few pages at a time of the manuscript and make lists, on Subway napkins, of all major words—meaning anything longer than four letters. Then, as soon as he gets a napkin-full, he'll slide it across the crumb-covered table at me, and I'll go to work on Google Translate. If it's a Basque word, then the definition will come up and I'll jot it down on the napkin. If we stump Google Translate, I'll just plain Google the word to see if I can figure it out. And if both of those things fail, then Kate will transfer the word to a whole new set of napkins known as the what-the-hell-language-is-this pile.

"Get it?" Kate finishes. "It's like, a dictionary on a pile of napkins. It's a *Napkinary*." She smiles at us. "And when we're done with it, we'll read the whole book from cover to cover, moving from major word to major word, consulting the Napkinary as we go. Hopefully we'll have found enough words to piece together the gist of what the book is saying."

Jay looks skeptical, but nods. He shoves the remnants of his sandwich aside. "I'm not sure it will work, but I don't have any better ideas."

"I can just see it now," Kate says, her wide eyes on some imaginary place above our heads. "Harvard and Brown will fight over us, the famous kids with the totally pathetic GPAs who discovered and translated a saint's lost manuscript. And we'll talk about how we did it all on Subway napkins. We'll be *heroes*."

"Yeah," Jay says flatly. "We'll go to Harvard. And then we'll fail calc once we get there. And get kicked out."

"No way," Kate says, carefully putting the napkins into a neat pile. "Noah will get us through math and—"

But she stops at the mention of Noah's name. We all look at each other. We don't have to say anything more. If the Napkinary will help us find him, then that's what we'll do.

SLOWLY, MIRACULOUSLY, THE NAPKINARY starts to take shape. The only trouble is that the pile of napkins Kate is filling with words I *can't* figure out is growing rapidly as well. My hope that we'll make sense of this thing is fading fast, but we keep going. We abuse the hell out of Subway's free refill policy to keep us all fully caffeinated for the project, and Kate occasionally goes up and orders a cookie or another bag of chips in an attempt to placate Crystal who looks pissed that we're using the shop as our makeshift library *and* draining the napkin supply.

Occasionally, I glance at the clock on the wall. It's almost six o'clock. I know we need to leave soon if we're going to maintain the lie at home, but I can't stop.

The absurdity of our extremely unorthodox Subway treatment of an ancient document is not lost on me. We all know that what we *should be* doing with this thing is driving it straight up to Case Western where Jay's dad was a prof, *not* pawing all over it with our sub-covered hands during amateur translation hour. But there's no way I'll let this book get taken away from us. Because I know what the snooty academics would do. They'd take ten million years to translate it and write esoteric articles about it for their boring journals. If the book *does* hold secrets about how to find my mom, I'd never find out. Plus, we wouldn't have any more clues about how to find Noah.

So we're keeping it. End of story.

But about an hour in, Kate and Jay start dragging. Jay takes forever to write down words and Kate keeps getting distracted by email coming through on her phone.

"OMG," she says, yawning. "It's almost six-thirty. We should start for home. I promised to be home by nine at the latest."

"Then let's just translate what we've got so far," I say. "We've got enough words to start—"

"We've got to *go*, Riley," Kate says. "If I'm home too late, I'll be grounded. And if I'm grounded, I'll miss junior prom. And if I miss junior prom, I'll fall into a depression. And if I fall into a depression, I'll start making a string of poor choices. I could get knocked up. Or marry the wrong guy. Who *knows* where it could lead?" She's trying to make me laugh, but this time I'm not taking the bait. Jay starts gathering up handfuls of the Napkinary.

"Fine." I sigh and begrudgingly help him gather napkins. "I mean, I understand that thinking about normal crap like prom can be a panacea of sorts, but still."

"OMG, I'm not even going to ask you to define panacea right now," Kate says as she gets up. "I'm hitting the girls' room. I'll meet you in the car."

I have no choice but to head out. My translation team has clearly had enough. The door bing-bongs again as I leave, and I make my way out to the car. I crawl in the backseat where I can spread out to work on the way home. As I wait for Jay and Kate, I look down at my phone and realize I should check in with Dad because we probably *will* be very late. So I text him and lie like crazy. I say we're still studying. That we may study until one or two in the morning. I say we're at Noah's house.

My jaw drops when he texts back.

Sounds good. Friends over. See you when you get home.

Friends? Dad has friends? At our house? As far as I know, he

hasn't hosted a party or had one single friend over since
Mom died. I stare at the text again to make sure I read it
right. *See you when you get home?* I mean, my dad is not the
Captain of the Watchful Parents League, but this is lax, even
for him. I'm still gaping at the screen when Kate comes back
to the car and buckles herself in the front passenger seat.

"Where's Jay?" I ask.

"Sure you want to know?"

"Crystal? Are you serious?" I ask.

She nods. "He stopped to say bye to the Sandwich Artist
Centerfold. I saw them talking when I came out of the
bathroom, and I was totally disgusted. I couldn't even look
at him."

I sigh and lie down in the back, curling into a ball on the
seat. I clutch the manuscript to my chest and close my eyes. I
can't figure out how to feel. I try to focus on what I'm sure I
want. I want to find my mom again; I want to know why I saw
her; I want to know where she is. And I want my heart to stop
hurting, to stop breaking all over.

But wanting all this, and picturing Jay in there hitting on
some strange girl—my heart shatters just a little bit more. If
he really doesn't know how I feel about him, then part of me
just wants to get up, storm back into Subway and tell him.
To just finally blurt it out and get it over with. On the other
hand, if he knows but still flirts with girls right in front of me,
especially with everything else that's going on—it's so epically
shitty that I can't even believe it. *Who does that?* His typical surprise act of decency that makes everything right better come
soon, and it better be momentous.

After an endless couple of minutes, the driver's side door
opens.

"No way," Kate says as Jay gets in. I sit up and open my eyes and see her grab a wadded-up napkin from his hand. Then she hands it to me, and I start to unfold it.

"Is it for the Basque pile or the we-have-no-clue pile?" I ask.

"Neither," Kate says, sighing.

She's right. It doesn't have Basque words on it. It has a phone number. And a distinctly English word: Crystal.

"You can just throw it away," Jay says. "And do I look okay to you?" He looks at Kate.

"Are you seriously worried about your looks right now?" she asks.

"No, I mean . . . do I look sick or something? Or pale?"

"Um," Kate says. She softens. "Well, maybe a little. Why?"

"I just felt so weird for a minute in there. I thought I was going to pass out or something. I didn't even want to talk to her. But I said 'hey' and then she was handing me her number—"

"Can we *please* just get out of Maryland?" I ask. "We're late; remember?"

"Yeah, sure," Jay says, eyeing me in the rearview mirror. He holds my eyes for just a minute, and gives me a look I can't decipher. Maybe it's *I'm sorry,* or maybe it's *I swear I like you back,* or maybe it's just *are you okay?* I can't tell, but I also can't stand to look in his eyes right now, so I don't. I look away and curl back into a ball.

Chapter 10

Don't Mess with the Nest.

Soon after we cross the Ohio border, I take the wheel again. The drive feels like it takes forever, but just staring straight ahead at the road calms me down a little. I drop Jay and Kate off at their houses and walk in my front door around midnight. I expect to see the living room dark. But I don't. The lights are all on. The sofa has a few blankets on it, and there are like four plates of half-eaten food on the coffee table. And the whole house smells like baking cinnamon rolls.

He's baking at midnight?

Maybe he knows what a wreck I am. Even though I tried so hard to hide it. He hears me come in and emerges from the kitchen, and I'm so glad to see him that I toss the manuscript on the entryway table and throw my arms around his neck. He grabs onto me and holds me tight, in a classic Serious Dad Hug. A Serious Dad Hug is definitely one of the greatest things on the planet. Even though I'm sixteen, and I'm totally supposed to be annoyed by stuff like this—right now, I love this hug. It feels like—*this idea that you could ever be alone, without someone who loves you—IT'S JUST NOT TRUE.*

"You okay?" he asks. "I was starting to worry. But thanks for the text. Hard study session?"

"Yeah, you could say that." I squeeze him a little tighter, grateful to be out of the car, part of me never wanting to leave this house ever again.

"Whoa," Dad says, eyeing the manuscript on the table. "What book is that?"

I walk over and pick it back up. "Nothing," I say. "Just an old book from the library. Um, we're learning how to find primary sources. For a project." I clutch it close to my chest and try to come up with something else to say about it if Dad digs any further, but then a rustling in the kitchen snaps me out of my thoughts.

"Oh," Dad says, worry clouding his blue eyes. "Some friends came by for a little dinner party and one is still . . ." His voice trails off.

A woman steps into the hallway. A *young* woman. Or at least, *way* younger than my dad. I'm crap at guessing ages, but from the looks of her vitamin-enriched hair, her nearly wrinkleless face, and her no-joke-totally-perfect boobs (even more perfect than Crystal's), she must be in her late twenties? Thirty at the most.

"Hi," she says sheepishly. She wipes a little baking flour off her shirt. "I'm Sammy."

She has a boy's name.

They're cooking together at midnight? Really?

Dad shifts on his feet, almost as clumsily as he did the day I told him I was growing a penis. "Riley, this is Sammy. Sammy, this is—"

"Riley." I jut out my hand. I give her a firm, respectable handshake. I'm no pageant queen, but my mother taught me basic manners, dammit. Plus, this must just be a neighbor I haven't met. Someone's mom. Someone's wife. She probably brought over some noodle salad to share because she had extra. It's what any good neighbor would do. Then she probably just stayed so she could . . . help Dad bake rolls at midnight.

"Sammy's an ornithologist," Dad explains, which explains absolutely nothing. "At the Cleveland Zoo. I inspected a house she wants to buy, and then she took me to the local bird club the other day. Such a great place. I never knew birds were so fascinating."

My dad's voice is so phony right now it's painful. This garbage about how a bird club is a thrill a minute is kind of making me want to upturn a bottle of Pepto-Bismol. And this woman is a real-estate client of his? I want to say something about all of this, I really do, but I don't know what.

And I *can't* say what's actually going through my mind because the only thing that's going through my mind—is my mom.

THE LAST LATE-NIGHT DINNER party my parents ever had, I was thirteen. They decided to host the holiday party for the real-estate company where my dad worked. I helped my mom get our house ready for *weeks*. And decorating with my mom was a slow, laborious process. She'd tell me what decorations to hang where and then ask me to describe how they looked. I must have moved our fake pine garland to fifty different places in the living room until she was happy.

The first half of the party seemed to go well. Our house was *full* of people and they were all babbling about how beautiful everything looked. There were real-estate agents, appraisers, inspectors, and even the owner of the company.

My dad trotted me over to her like a prize calf at the state fair and made me shake her hand. But then I noticed that my dad was beaming as he introduced us. And he wasn't beaming in an I'm-so-proud-of-my-daughter kind of way, he was beaming at *her*.

I mean, I have to give it to him; she was pretty. And super stylish. She had on this clingy sweater-dress thing and knee-high boots. And her hair was long and perfectly curled at the ends. But still, I didn't like the look on my dad's face. Something about it wasn't quite right.

Then I caught sight of my mom. And she looked kind of dull, like someone had just turned off a light inside her. I watched as she slipped out of the living room and went upstairs. As soon as I could get away from the big-shot sweater-dress lady, I followed her.

I found her in her bedroom, standing in front of her closet, holding her annual half glass of wine in one hand and gently touching some hanging clothes with the other.

"What are you doing?" I asked.

"Oh, nothing," she said. She pulled a hanger out of the closet that held a shirt and a pair of pants. "These are some of my old nurse scrubs, right?"

"Yes," I said.

"I thought so," she said with a big smile, her damaged eyes drifting. "Which ones are they? I can't tell—are these windmills or lollipops?"

They weren't either one. They were covered with plain polka-dots, but I didn't have the heart to tell her.

"Windmills," I said.

"Some of my favorites," she said wistfully. "I think I was a really good nurse, you know? I really think I was."

My mind went blank for a minute as I searched the

darkness in my brain for something to say. "I'm not that impressed with that woman," I blurted out. "I mean, she runs a real-estate office. *Big deal.* And she looks pretty cheesy if you ask me."

"Your father seems to be impressed with her," Mom said quietly. She felt along in the closet for the place to hang the scrubs up. "I could hear it in his voice. When he introduced her to you."

I walked over to the closet and helped her guide the hanger into place. "Well," I said slowly. "You have a career, too. You're a mom."

My mother reached for me. She was a little off with her aim, so I quickly stepped sideways into her arms. "Unfortunately, a lot of people don't see it that way," she said as she gave me a gentle squeeze. "It just . . . I don't know—it doesn't seem to count."

Even at thirteen, I thought to do the quick math in my head.

Give birth + give up your life to raise a kid + get no respect = remind me not to have kids when I grow up.

HOW UNFAIR IS IT that I'm now standing in our living room in the middle of my dad's late-night date with a PhD ornitholo-whatever? Thankfully, before Dad can tell me more about how *fascinating* this bird-woman Sammy apparently is, the oven alarm bings.

"Rolls are ready!" he says in this totally obnoxious sing-songy voice I swear I've never heard before. He looks grateful for the distraction and runs into the kitchen.

And that's when I see it: the look in Sammy's eyes.

It instantly reminds me of this article I read in *National*

Geographic about filial cannibalism—when animals eat their young. Turns out there are many reasons why animals do it. Sometimes new female mates don't want the earlier family to survive. The new animal "wife" wants only *her* children to prosper, to be the only carriers of her new "husband's" genes. There were even pictures. In one, a house finch sat in a nest, eyeing a brood of young birds. In the next, she was attacking one of them. Even though the second picture was the violent one, the first was more disturbing. There was something about the way the finch eyed the baby bird the moment before she attacked. Her eyes were a hard, homicidal black.

And that's exactly how this woman is looking at me.

It's there for only the briefest of moments, but I *swear it's there.* She's eyeing me with that dark, cold look, like she wants to eat me, revise history, stamp out any evidence of my dad's previous partners.

And that's when I know.

This woman is dating my dad.

I want to scream. I want to vomit. But then I want to be silent. I want to be more silent than silent. I want to fade into the wallpaper, become just another paisley bean-shaped dot on a wall of paisley bean-shaped dots. I'm overwhelmed with the feeling that I've been replaced. (Which is kind of sick I know, because it's not like *I'm* my dad's wife or anything.) But still. I'm a representative of the *first* administration, the genetic offshoot of the *first* family.

A word comes to mind: *ousted.* I've been ousted, a victim of a bloodless coup. I leave the house for one single night, and I come back to find the palace ransacked, our flag burned, a new family crest being painted on the throne.

But in an instant I summon the numbness. I don my I'm-fine armor as Dad comes back from the kitchen.

"I'm fine," I say, nearly shouting the answer to a question no one asked. And then I take off up the stairs. When I reach the top, I look down at the new couple, at their shocked faces, at the how-do-we-handle-this confusion in their eyes. "Totally. And completely. FINE."

And with that, I go to my room and slam the door.

But the minute I'm alone, it all really hits me. I feel like I did back in the cave; my lungs can't fill with enough air. I feel abandoned, left behind with my messed-up life as my father takes off to a shiny new future. And I want my mom so badly, I can barely stay standing up. That old, familiar ache fills my body. I know it's grief. I've lived with it for over two years, and I know it so well. It's like a roommate who never leaves the house, like the brother I never had. Sometimes he's quiet. Sometimes he rages. Sometimes he hides under your bed, silent and scattered like dust. And sometimes, you almost forget he's there.

Almost.

Mom. I need you.

I toss the manuscript on the bed, terrified I'll never be able to decipher it. That I'll never see her again, that I'll never get another chance . . .

My dad knocks on my door. My heart pounds almost as loud as he does. I inform him that I am NOT answering, that I am NOT coming out.

"Riley." Muffled, through the wood. "Please? Can we talk about this?"

"No."

"How about some beef stew?"

"NO."

"Late night cinnamon rolls? They're just out of the oven."

"*NO.*"

So much for the numbness and the armor. I flop down on my bed and stare at the ceiling, willing away the lump in my throat that manages to make yet another appearance. A few minutes pass, and I hear Dad plod back downstairs. I hear him apologize to Sammy for my behavior. I can't hear Sammy's response, but I bet she's saying all the right kissing-up-to-the-new-boyfriend-who-has-a-teenager things.

It's okay, Ben. This is all so new. And the poor thing lost her mother.

I stare up at the glow-in-the-dark stars stuck to my ceiling and at my overhead light, a glowing plastic red and white balloon. And then I glance at the puppy lamp on the bedside table. My heart sinks when I think back to my mom and me making plans to redecorate the room. I remember holding a book of wallpaper samples, trying my best to describe to her what they looked like.

"This one, is, um, little flowers. With dots below each one. In green," I said.

"What shade of green?" Mom asked.

"Like, dark green."

"Pine or hunter?"

There's a difference? "Pine," I said, knowing I couldn't tell pine from hunter any more than I could ace a chem test.

Now, I feel sick looking at the childish lamp and the overhead light and at the wallpaper we never changed. And suddenly, I'm overwhelmed with an urge to get rid of it all. To rip everything out, to just let go, move on, grow up from a world of balloon lights to walls of distinguished hunter green. *If Dad is going to move on, shouldn't I?*

I eye the overhead balloon light and the rusty screw that holds it in place. And I feel a twinge. I can't locate it; all I know is that it's somewhere deep inside me. *Go ahead. Get rid of it.* I quietly open my bedroom door and make my way to the garage to find a screwdriver and a stepladder. I haul them upstairs, being unbelievably stealthy as I pass the kitchen. I make it up to my room undetected and enter it like it's a war zone: *me vs. sentimental attachment to the past.*

I unfold the ladder, click the steps into place and climb up. I look at the screw holding the balloon light together and go at it with an almost violent determination. I work quickly and pull the screw out of its socket. The light cover comes next, and I hold it in my hands like hard-won war booty.

And then I hear another knock at the door.

"Go away, Dad," I mutter. I squint in the harsh light of the now-exposed light bulb. I hear him mumble something on the other side of the door. "Seriously. *Go away.*"

But he says something again, too quietly. So I grip the balloon light cover and make my way down the stepladder, angrier with every step. I swing the door open, praying that it's just my Dad on the other side and that Sammy isn't standing behind him in all her perfectness.

It's neither of them.

It's Noah. Standing in my doorway with his NASA-blue eyes and in a Milky Way galaxy T-shirt that says YOU ARE HERE. And he looks tired. *Really* tired.

Chapter 11

Tell Me Everything.

I drop the balloon light cover and pull him into my room. I wrap my arms around him and hold tight.

"I'm so glad you're okay," I whisper over his shoulder. But then I pull back and look into his eyes, his pupils small black knots of worry. "Wait. You're okay? Right?"

He nods. "I'm okay."

But it's totally unconvincing. And with that, everything comes flooding back: the 14,000 unanswered texts, the mad dash to Maryland, the terrifying trip into the cave to look for him. I want to sock him in the stomach.

"Where *were* you?" I hiss. It's a struggle to keep my voice down.

He looks at me sheepishly, stuffs his hands in his jeans pockets. "Would you kill me if I said I can't tell you?"

"Yes. Absolutely yes."

"Well, I can't. I promised."

"Promised *who*?"

"Promised *whom*, and I can't tell you that either." He sits down on my bed. I've never seen him look so tired, so stressed.

"Did you seriously just show up in my room after midnight, dodge my question, *and* correct my grammar?"

He flashes me a quick and silent *I'm sorry.* "And I was going to text you from the front porch so you could sneak me in, but all the curtains were open and the lights were on, so your dad saw me come up the porch steps. Then he just let me in, like I didn't just show up at midnight. He seemed a little . . . distracted."

"Yeah, I'm aware. He's on a date. But just tell me—" I stop as a warm breeze fills the room, and I look at the large square of blackness that is my bedroom window. It's cranked open to let the night air in and a nearly full moon hangs in the sky. I think about all the research in Noah's room, the stuff about my mom, the stuff about the cross necklace. I sit cross-legged next to him on the bed and look directly into his eyes.

"Tell me what you know, Noah."

He looks away and doesn't say anything. It's like he's waiting for something. Finally, he talks. "All I can tell you right now is—" he starts but stops again, hesitating.

"Tell me," I plead, feeling my hazel eyes burn bright. I'm told they get more green than brown when I'm mad or when I really, really want something. And I bet they're near a deep emerald at this point.

"Just . . . pay attention," he says.

"*I am.*"

"No. I mean, that's all I can tell you right now. To pay attention. To every idea you have. If you feel like doing something, stop and ask what it feels like in your body. Does it feel like a splat, like a drop of water hitting a stone? Or does it feel soft, like water hitting a sponge?"

"What the hell? Sponges? You're talking about sponges now? You sound crazy. You know that, right?" I scoot away from him on the bed. "Just tell me why your room was full of stuff about my mom, stuff that you got from *here*. Just tell me—"

"Okay, okay," he says, taking my hand and gently pulling me close again. A shiver crawls over my skin; his touch is so soft. It *is* like water on a sponge; its warmth spreads from its source. "Don't bail on me. I was making something." He looks straight at me as he says it, and in the harsh light from the bare overhead bulb, I see that same old trust-me look in his eyes, that same mix of worry and care I saw when he stood on my front porch with a handful of wildflowers from the side of the road on Mom's first deathiversary. I see the Noah who always tells me everything. "Remember when I got in trouble at the start of the year?"

"For hiding week-old burritos in Mr. Schink's ceiling?"

"Yeah. That." He cracks a half-smile. "Which was kind of awesome, you have to admit. I mean, it took them like *two weeks* to figure out where the smell was coming from—"

"Yeah, yeah. Prank brilliance. Keep talking."

"Right. Sorry," he says. "So remember the old counselor in Back on Track, Ms. Thomas? The one who left right before winter break? Well, when I got caught for the burrito thing she gave me this whole lecture about how I was 'acting out' because I hadn't really 'dealt with my grief.' And she gave me a really stupid assignment. I had to make a collage about Cam. Fill it with stuff he liked, quotes, pictures. To like, honor him. And then I had to make one about the people my friends lost, too. She said it would help get me out of myself. To think of others."

I picture the incredibly not-artistic Noah, busy with lefty scissors and glue sticks, putting together a tribute to my mom. And I bet my eyes are fading from hot green back to hazel.

"That's not such a bad assignment," I say softly. "It's really kind of nice, actually."

"I wanted to make it personal, so that's why I snuck in here. It was stupid and wrong, I know. But it came from a good place, I swear. I was going to give you the one about your mom on her next deathiversary and explain it all," he says. "But I'm guessing it looked super creepy when you found all that stuff in my room . . ."

"The creepiest."

He picks at a few stray threads that hang from a hole in the knee of his jeans. "Anyway, that assignment. That's how it all started. When I got to the collage for Jay, about his dad, I started reading about his dad's research. And I found all of Saint Ignatius's theories about spirits. And I thought that maybe if I could learn enough, I could find a way to talk to—" His voice breaks a little; one of the threads from his jeans comes loose in his hand.

"To talk to Cam?"

"Yeah," he says. He looks up at my ceiling. Or maybe beyond it. "You know. To ask him why. Why he left us. Why he did it. And then when you saw your mom, I thought for sure I had a shot to see him again. You know?"

"Yeah. I know." My heart shudders, dying a tiny little death for him. I uncross my legs, scoot close. I lean against him and lay my head on his shoulder. I want to know where he's been, where he took the cross; I want to know everything he knows, but I don't want to push. Not now. Not when he feels like this, not when I'm terrified he'll run off again. So we sit there like that, in the quiet, holding that thing between us that only survivors know—an ache to cheat death, to reach across, to ask what you forgot to ask, to say what you should've said, to see the one you've lost for even one second more.

"Wait," he says, squinting up at the bare bulb. He gets up and flips the light switch, plunging us into darkness. He sits back down beside me. "Look up."

I do, and as my eyes adjust, I see the scattered glow-in-the-dark stars on my ceiling. They're burning a bright neon green.

"You know your plastic star constellations are *jacked*," he says softly. "The Big Dipper isn't even in the right place. Is that corner supposed to be north?"

I smile a little. "I don't know. I stuck them up there when I was seven. What's a proto-astronomer charge for fixing plastic stars?"

"*Super* pricey."

Moonlight streams through the window, coating my room in silvery light. I look down at the comforter we're sitting on and run my hand over the pattern of balloons dancing across the cotton below us. And suddenly, I wish I hadn't torn down my balloon light; I don't want to get rid of my old, childish things that Mom gave me. I want to cover my room in balloons from floor to ceiling; I want to float away like they can—light and free, full of color, empty of memories.

"I'm sorry I scared you," Noah says. "And I think—" He stops and looks straight at me. But instead of finishing his sentence, he leans in. So close I can feel his light breath.

But then it happens.

For just a heartbeat of a moment, something flickers in Noah's eyes. Like a shadow passing over him. I blink and then blink again. But I still see it: flashes of someone else in his place, someone I've never seen before.

And then it's over. Just like with my mom in the store, Noah is himself again.

My heart rattles away in my chest like my ribcage is a jail and it's desperate for the key. Noah looks worried and confused as I scramble off the bed, nearly getting tangled up in the comforter as I push off the mattress.

"I'm sorry," he says. "I shouldn't have come here like this . . ."

I don't hear the end of his sentence. Because I'm already out my bedroom door, racing down the stairs, blinking in the bright light of the hallway, coaching myself: *Breathe. Breathe. Breathe.*

I run so fast, I miss the last stair and stumble onto the landing in front of the kitchen. I glance inside, but Sammy and Dad haven't noticed me. Dad has got the blender on now, making who-knows-what, and Sammy says something that makes him smile like crazy. I turn and keep going. I dash out the front door, take the porch steps two at a time, and then pound across the grass as fast as my legs will carry me. I hit the street, and I'm mildly aware of the pavement below my feet, the street lights whizzing past, as I run and run and run. Finally, lungs aching, I have to stop. I bend over, put my hands on my knees and gasp for breath.

Then I hear footsteps.

Noah is racing down the street after me. And I can't run anymore. I don't have enough air or strength left. I'm so afraid of what or who I'll see when he reaches me, and I put my hands over my face.

"Riley," Noah says, putting a hand on my back. "What happened back there? Tell me."

I drop my hands a little. And it's just Noah. He's himself and no one else. "I saw . . ." I begin, still a little breathless.

"Someone else?"

"Yes," I say, nodding in the darkness. "And you have to tell me everything you know. Now. *Everything.*"

I can feel the pity he has for me. I can see it in his eyes as he nods and hear it in his voice as he says the thing I've been waiting for:

"I know why you saw your mom."

Chapter 12

Goodnight Kiss

Two houses down, a porch light snaps on and a dog starts to bark.

"Come on," Noah says, taking my hand. We hurry down the street, back to my house. The driveway light is on and Sammy's red Jetta is still parked on the street.

"I don't want to go back in there," I say, pointing at the Jetta. "She's still here."

Noah starts for the wooden swing on our front porch, but I let go of his hand and head for my car in the driveway. I try the driver's side door and it opens. I guess I was so tired when I got back from Maryland I forgot to lock it.

"Get in," I say as I slip into the driver's seat. Noah climbs in on the passenger side.

"Are you sure you're ready for this?" he asks.

I nod.

"Okay." He angles his seat back so he's almost fully reclining. I do the same. It's too dark to really see him, so I reach up and pull the sunroof cover open, letting the moonlight fill the car. As I lean back in my seat, I catch the tremble in my hands. I close my eyes, willing the fear away. All I can hear is our breath. I look over at him, silently demanding: *Tell me everything.*

"The research I did," he says slowly. "About Saint Ignatius. One of his major theories is called the *discernment of spirits.*"

Just then, I catch movement out of the corner of my eye. My stomach twists as Dad and Sammy emerge on the front porch of our house. They're holding hands. I close my eyes and wish that I was a beautiful red balloon and could float up through the sunroof, high into the sky. Higher and higher, too far away to see hot-girl Jettas and parental PDA.

I open my eyes. "Put your seat down more," I say, cranking mine as far back as it will go. "Or they'll see us."

"They'll think we're—"

"Exactly," I say, cutting Noah off before he can finish his sentence. We hunker down as low as we can. We turn on our sides, facing each other.

"Go on," I say. "I learned a little about this already. Looking for you, actually."

He blinks and flashes an apologetic smile. "So, the discernment of spirits is one of the foundations of the Jesuit Society, and Ignatius wrote about it in his famous book. During his enlightenment, when he wore his cross—the same cross Jay's dad found, the same cross that you all wore—he had this flash and was shown that spirits influence us all the time. Good ones and bad ones. They toy with our insides when we're trying to make important decisions. They give us chills, a sense of shock, or really strong urges to do one thing or the other."

Noah stops and sneaks a peek at the front porch. But I know Dad and Sammy have moved. Now they're sitting on our porch swing that's almost directly in front of us. They swing and swing. Even through the closed car doors, I can hear the chains creak. Back and forth. Back and forth. Finally I have to look for myself.

Sammy has put her head on Dad's shoulder. They still haven't noticed us.

"*Keep going,*" I say to Noah in a whispery hiss. "Ignore them."

"Okay. So Ignatius wrote down directions. Tips on how to figure out which spirit is moving us: a good one or a bad one. We have to pay attention to how decisions feel in our body. Sometimes a spirit gives you a splat, like water hitting a stone. A little sign to go a different way. But other times it feels different, like water hitting a sponge." He stops and sighs. He looks frustrated by trying to explain. "Anyway, that's what his famous book was about: how different spirits feel when they are in us. That's part of what he ran around teaching people: how to discern spirits."

"I don't get it," I say. "What does this have to do with my mom?"

Noah looks up at the night sky through the sunroof. "I'll think of a way to explain." He looks directly at the bright moon, squinting. "Okay. Think about a decision you've made. Maybe one you regret?"

"Um," I say slowly, more confused than anything else. I don't have to say anything; Noah can see the disbelief on my face.

"Just go with me," Noah says. "Think back."

So I do. And I know right away what decision I regret. It's the worst choice I've ever made, the last night I saw my mother alive. After our fight, I watched her grab the car keys and head for the front door. I felt such a strong urge to tell her to stop, to not go, that it was too dangerous. I wanted to shout that I was sorry about our fight, about what I said. I wanted to tell her that I loved her. But I didn't. I just stood there and watched her go.

"The night my mom died," I say slowly. "After our fight. I didn't try to stop her when she left with the car keys."

"And when you didn't do anything . . . how did it feel in your body?"

I hate thinking about that night; I wish I could forget it, but I can't. I know exactly how I felt as I watched my mom head for the door.

"It wasn't a splat, exactly. But sort of like that. I had this sinking feeling." I stare down at the darkened dashboard, the dials resting on empty, on zero miles an hour. "And then I wanted to say something. *Stop her.* That's what was running through my mind. *Stop her.* And I was covered in tons of chills. Tons."

Noah nods slowly. "According to Saint Ignatius, those chills weren't coming from you. A spirit was there that night, influencing you. Giving you those sinking feelings. Those chills. It was trying to get you to . . ."

He doesn't finish his sentence because he can see that I get it. I get it all too well.

A spirit was there that night, trying to get me to save my mother's life.

The silence in the car is as unbearable as the thoughts roaring in my head. I look through the windshield fog and see Dad and Sammy again on the swing. Except now they're kissing. And kissing and kissing. Watching them feels like a swift kick to my ribcage. How *could* he? I squeeze my eyes shut, trying to block them out, trying to focus on my mother, to put it all together.

"A good spirit tried to get me to stop her," I whisper. "Or maybe an evil one showed up and convinced me to stay quiet."

I open my eyes and see Noah's face get a little melty with sadness. "Yes," he says. "I'm so sorry but . . . yes."

My breath comes fast and shallow, like I can't pull it in or push it out. *I ignored the urge to stop her.* And went with the urge to keep my mouth shut. I went with the wrong spirit. And my mother ran out the door and got behind the wheel. My mother died because I wasn't paying attention, because I'm so bad at figuring out what I'm supposed to do.

Just like I thought. *It's all my fault.*

"That's Saint Ignatius's theory, at least," Noah says. I can tell he's searching for something to say to make me feel better. "And that part is no secret. It was in his published version, that spirits give us 'interior motions,' influence us when we make important decisions." He pauses and then looks up through the sunroof again. "And I think that's why you saw your mom. Because you wore Saint Ignatius's cross. You can see what he could."

My thoughts pop like firecrackers, each one a jolt. I fight to stay clear. "So I saw my mom's spirit," I whisper slowly. "In the store. She was inside a living person." I look at Noah again. "Mom was . . . trying to influence her?" He nods. "But *why?* What was she doing? I mean, the woman was looking at bubble bath."

Noah shakes his head. He bites his lip, hesitating.

I glance at my Dad and Sammy again.

He's running his hand up Sammy's shirt. I'm desperate to look away, but I can't because now I catch a flicker where Dad sits, faint in the porch light. Dad's salt and pepper hair flashes with red; his skin is suddenly pale. I don't recognize the man I see in his place. "It's happening again," I say, pointing. "To my Dad. Do you see it? There must be a spirit—"

"I haven't worn the cross," Noah interrupts, not listening. "I was told not to."

Who told you not to? But I don't ask him out loud, because I get hit with a horrible thought. I think back to the old fashioned bride I saw outside the gas station on our way to Maryland. How she flickered inside that homeless woman. How she asked for my help. I look at my dad and then at Noah.

"What do they need our help with? The spirits?" I ask, frantic now. "Does my mom need help?"

Noah stares into my eyes. "I don't know that part," he says. "Remember what's etched on the back of the cross? There's *magis*—more—to Ignatius's spirit theory that no one knows. That's what Ignatius hid in his original book. The one he never published, the one he hid from the Roman Inquisitors. Some scholars have guessed that it's about what the spirits are up to. Why they're messing with us in the first place. And that's what we have to find out."

"So we need the original manuscript," I say.

"Exactly. And Jay's dad knew where it was. It's in a cave. In Maryland. But he left it there. On purpose."

"Where do you think we looked for you first?" I ask, my voice shaky. "We went there. We *found* it. I have it. And it's up in my room."

Noah blinks several times. "You . . . you *what?*"

I nod. "But don't get your hopes up. It's impossible to read . . . we couldn't even figure out the language."

He looks away from me, then back. "We have to try. If you really did find it." I can hear the panic in his voice, the panic I can feel. It floods through me like liquid concrete, threatening to harden and swallow me whole.

But what if we can't figure it out?

I thought there could be nothing worse than spending the rest of my life always looking for my mother, always checking strangers in the grocery store, random cars on the highway, never knowing when or if I might see her again. Never getting to say I'm sorry. But there *is* something worse. And it's this: Knowing that I wrecked my mom's life, and that now I'm somehow wrecking her afterlife, too. Because if she needs help, I can't figure out how to give it to her.

Air. I NEED AIR.

I throw open the car door and stagger out, pulling in a long, deep breath. The chains on the porch swing rattle as Dad sees me. He bolts out of Sammy's arms, eyes wide.

"Riley? What are you doing in your car?"

Just then, Noah steps out of the passenger side of the fogged-up Wagon.

"Oh," Dad says. He freezes. Slumps a little. I can feel his embarrassment in the dark and see the confusion on his face in the dim porch light. I can tell he's shocked, but not because he thinks he just caught me making out in the driveway. The way he looks at me and then at Noah, it's more like . . . *But I thought you liked Jay?*

I storm up the porch stairs.

"Don't. Say . . ." I pause, still half-breathless. I look at Sammy as she adjusts her shirt on the porch swing. "A word."

UPSTAIRS IN MY ROOM, alone with Noah, I keep expecting Dad to knock. To hear his footsteps pounding up the stairs. There's nothing. Not a peep of protest. Maybe he's back on the porch swing with Sammy. I guess when your teenage daughter catches you making out with someone she didn't even know *existed* until an hour ago, you can't exactly negotiate house rules from a position of strength.

So I focus on my mother. On what matters. I show Noah the manuscript and explain how we found it, making sure to describe in extra detail how scary it was, to make him feel extra-guilty, which he *should*. And he does. But he still doesn't tell me where he went instead. After that, I tell him about our ingenious Napkinary.

Then I realize there's a big problem: I can't find the napkins.

"Shit," I say, rifling through my room. "Jay must have taken the napkins home with him." Noah lies on the floor, propped up on his elbows, paging through the manuscript.

"We looked up the history of this thing after we found it," I explain. "We think it's his original. The one Ignatius never published. His signature and the date are on the last page."

"*Exactamundo*," Noah says. His eyes are bright and he sits up, cross-legged, flipping through the wrinkled pages as delicately as he can. "The Vatican demanded to see what he was teaching people. The Inquisitors threw him in jail while they reviewed his book. Except he didn't give them this one." Noah taps a finger on the front cover. "He gave them a watered-down Latin version made by his secretary."

"Saints have secretaries?"

"Yes. And they don't mess with Inquisitors." He keeps turning the pages, eyeing every one. "The theory is that Ignatian relics, like the cross and manuscript, were sent over with Andrew White. The Jesuit who founded the Maryland colony."

I shake my head as I watch him. I'm still stunned by how much he knows. "We didn't get very far with the Napkinary," I admit. "We were only able to translate the major words on the first few pages."

"That's okay," Noah says. "Because we don't need the first few pages. In fact, we don't need the majority of them. We just need these." He stops near the end and points at one of the final pages. I lie down next to him and peer over his shoulder. "I've read the published version cover to cover. And this has all the same sections, plus one extra." At the top of the page is the word MAGIS, written large. "There's no Magis section in the published Latin text."

Below the word MAGIS, there's a paragraph and then a lot of blank space. And then a sentence:

Nos omnostria sumus . . .

The sentence doesn't end with another word. It ends with scribbles.

"What is that?" I ask.

"No idea," Noah says, squinting. "Looks like medieval doodling."

"Is it a symbol?"

"Googling," Noah says, reaching for his phone. "But I've never seen one that looks anything like this. The main Jesuit seal has Greek letters and a cross. And I've been through all of Jay's dad's stuff. No symbols like this in there, either."

I grab my laptop off my dresser and enter *Nos omnostria sumus* into Google Translate. It spits it back out at me and guesses that the language is Finnish, just like it did in Subway when it had no clue what the word meant. I move on to the symbol. I Google phrases like *Ignatian symbols, Jesuit symbols,* and *Catholic symbols.* And a lot of stuff comes up, but it's all generic: the basic sign for the Jesuit order and a description of it. I stare at the symbol for the Jesuit Society.

It's a sun with a cross and letters inside—the Greek letters iota, eta, and an *S,* which it says is probably a Latin approximation for the Greek letter sigma. Three nails hover underneath the letters and form a *V* shape. I look back at the manuscript. The squiggles don't look anything like the Jesuit seal.

I go back to web results and search again using Google Scholar. I open the first academic article that comes up. It lists super basic Catholic symbols like crosses, flaming hearts, and fish, complete with lame commentary like, "Most world religions rely heavily on symbolism."

Thank you, Professor Obvious, PhD.

"I don't think I've ever said what I'm about to say," I say slowly, still pecking away at my laptop. "Nor did I ever think it would be uttered by any human ever. But . . . the Internet isn't helping."

We stare at each other, blinking.

"I know what we need," I say, arching an eyebrow at him.

"Librarians," he answers, reading my mind. "I know, I know, my specialty."

Again, I feel warmth, like water across the surface of a sponge. But there's more to it. Is a spirit present here now, trying to tell me something? But what? If anything, I hope it means we're at least on the right track.

"Know of any libraries open at 1 A.M. on a Sunday night?" he asks, snapping me out of my reverie.

I enter *Cleveland Public Library* into the search box. The Internet helps with that, at least. "The main branch of the CPL opens at 8:30 A.M. tomorrow. We can get Kate and Jay on the way. And it's not like any of our teachers will be shocked if the Back on Track foursome skip school."

"Not in the least." Noah takes a deep breath and stretches out on his back. I do the same. And I'm not sure how much longer we lie like that, staring up at my fake bedroom sky. But I know we fall asleep at some point, because the last thing I remember is looking up at my not-in-the-north North Star and thinking, just before I close my eyes:

Mom. I'm coming.

Chapter 13

Mini-Mart Meaning

At 7 A.M., I text Jay and Kate and let them know I've found Noah. That we need to skip school and that we'll pick them up in an hour. I add strict instructions that they are *not* to push Noah about where he's been or who he's talked to. *He* knows more than he's telling me, and *I* know that we can't afford to have him bail again. I can't live with the stress.

We get Jay first; he's ready and out of the house faster than he ever has been before. He opens the back passenger door and slides in. Then he reaches up front to give me the fist-bump handshake.

"Where in the *hell* have you been, dude?" he says to Noah before he even completes the fadeaway.

So much for the promise Jay made me. I shoot him an angry look in the rearview mirror.

"Spent the night at Riley's," Noah says with a smirk. I can tell he knows how that sounds. I can also tell he likes it.

"It's not like *that*," I say. "He crashed at my place when he came home. We were trying to read the manuscript."

"I meant where were you in the global sense," Jay

grumbles. "Like, where did you go and where the hell is my dad's cross?"

"Jay," I warn. "Come on . . ."

"I'm aware that you are going to hate me for saying this," Noah says. "But I really can't tell you. I promised. But the cross is safe, okay? Trust me."

I shoot Jay another look in the rearview mirror, which clearly and unmistakably says: *Don't screw this up.*

Jay shakes his head, leaning back in his seat.

We get Kate next. She races out of the house, her long black hair still wet from the shower. She clutches her backpack in one hand and her makeup bag in the other.

"OMG-where-were-you?" she says to Noah, breathless as she gets in the backseat.

"Don't ask," Jay says. "We're not allowed to know."

"Are you *serious?*" Kate looks at me in the rearview. "I thought he could at least tell us—" She stops when I give her my best trust-me eyes.

"Let's all just chill," I announce. "And get to the library. The CPL. We know what part of the manuscript we need to figure out, and maybe they can help us there."

"Did you remember to grab it?" Noah asks.

"It's in my bag. In the way-back," I say.

"This is all so unbelievable," Kate says. "Thank god I'm stocked up on candy."

I realize as I speed off that I completely agree. It is all so unbelievable. Every single thing about what's going on between the four of us, and why. Because none of us has a freaking clue.

WE'VE DONE THIS BEFORE. Well, the skipping school part. Not the Cleveland library part. And we've already perfected the strategy. The best thing to do is to just not show up for first period. Parents don't get called until the beginning of second period while the school secretary waits to see if you are going to show up late. So that means just before the second period bell, I have to text my dad at work and tell him that I'm sick. And that I'm on my way home. So by the time the school calls, my dad can inform them that I'm sick today. Then I always wait about fifteen minutes or so, text Dad at work again, and tell him I'm home safe and sound and tucked in bed. We all do it. It works every time.

"Somebody set the second period bell alarm on a phone," I instruct. "So we don't forget to text home." No one confirms, but I see Kate whip out her cell in the back.

It takes about twenty minutes to get to the CPL. The silence hangs thick among us. Jay leans into the front seat and turns on the radio. He scans through station after station and hits a county song. Two dudes, twanging about horses.

"Ooh. Stay there, stay there," Kate says. "Love this song."

Jay and I exchange a smirk in the mirror, his crazy-beautiful brown eyes beaming in the light that pours through the sunroof. I feel that little rush I sometimes do when I look directly at him. I force my eyes back to the road. But then I realize something, too: that rush, it's fleeting, but I should pay attention. Like Noah said . . .

An idea hits me.

If Noah is right about what St. Ignatius figured out—that good and evil spirits sometimes inhabit us, toy with our insides, give us urges to do one thing or the other—then maybe I should just follow every single urge and whim I have. If these spirits are trying to get me to do something, if they need my help, or if one will guide me to my mom again, then surely if I follow through with every idea that comes to me, one of them is *bound* to be what a spirit wants me to do. Eventually, some urge I follow will be the right one and might help me figure this out. I should just throw caution to the wind: *think it, do it.*

As if that were the person I am. It's almost funny. If there were a lighted marquee on my forehead it would read the most unlikely of announcements: *Hold onto your hats. I'm about to do every single thing that pops into my head.*

"This is taking forever," Noah complains. He's fidgeting in his seat, and his brow is furrowed. We need to keep him calm and happy. I glance over at him, try to read him. I wonder if he's thinking about life after death, about the chance to see Cam again. I remember when he said that Jay and I don't have a corner on the pain market, just because we're the only two in the group who have lost parents.

"Penny for your thoughts." I try to keep my tone light as I turn on my blinker and move into the passing lane.

Noah forces a quick smile. "Beef sticks vs. beef jerky. Which is better?" he asks.

"*Beef jerky?* At a time like this?" Kate says from the back. Noah throws me a sideways grin.

That's when the screaming starts.

It's incomprehensible, and all at once. Kate is shrieking and climbing into the way-back. Jay scrambles after her. Noah just looks confused, staring at me, and saying over and over, "What the hell? What the hell?"

And that's when I notice my arms . . . they're covered in chills. Absolutely covered. I have goose bumps on top of goose bumps. And I know. The screaming is about something inside this car—or rather, who's inside *me*. A spirit. One must be here.

"OMG, OMG," Kate stammers.

"Slow your roll, Riley. Slow your roll," is all Jay can manage.

I look down at the speedometer. He's right; I'm speeding like crazy.

"The hell? Seriously. The hell?" Noah says. "Do you guys see—"

"Yes," Kate squeaks. "In Riley. Right now. I saw just a glimpse. But it was someone. Someone else."

And then I realize I'm still going too fast. And that the country music is still blasting out of the speakers. The song is about bird dogs and gigging frogs.

I know I should totally be freaking out like everyone else, but I'm not. Instead of thinking about spirits, or my mom, or even how the sound of my friends freaking out is starting to give me a dull thudding headache, I'm thinking about the line in the country song about gigging frogs. It's like I've disassociated from my body, from the car, from the whole situation just to survive it. I'm thinking about how I don't have a clue what it means—to *gig* a frog. Does it involve *throwing* frogs? *Juggling* frogs? Maybe *chasing* them? Or is it something more sinister, like hitting them with a mallet or something? And then I start trying to conjugate the verb "to gig." *She will gig, she is gigging, she gigged? Or she gugged?*

But then, unfortunately, my strange sense of calm fades, and I attempt to pay attention to what this spirit might want me to do. As much as I try to notice what it's trying to make me feel, what the chills might be pointing me to, I can't. I start to panic.

"It's okay," Noah whispers. "The spirit is trying to get you to do something, Riley. Or to feel something. *Think.* Clear your head. What is it?"

It's hard enough just to focus on driving without getting us all killed. "I don't know. I can't think. I can't—I can't— " I'm stuttering.

"What are you talking about, Noah?" Kate says. "What do you mean a spirit is trying to get her to do something?"

"I'll explain later," Noah says. He turns and faces me. "Just keep your eyes on the road. Don't wreck. There are Ignatian spirit tests. What—"

"Wait," Jay interrupts. "I remember this. My dad talked about spirit tests . . . *discernment.*" He stops, putting it all together. "*Of course.*" Jay leans up in the front seat. "What were we talking about right before the spirit showed up? Maybe that's a clue about what it wants?"

"Can someone tell me what's going on?" Kate asks, her voice shaky.

"Spirits inhabit us," Noah says. "They try to influence us to do one thing or another. I think because you guys wore the cross, that's what you're seeing: the spirits at work."

"Jerky," Jay says. "We were talking about eating jerky. Maybe that's it. Maybe it wants Riley to eat beef jerky?"

I want to tell him he's an idiot, but I'm so scared, my mouth isn't working right.

"It's worth a try," Jay says. "Pull off. This exit has a gas station."

That, I do. I spin the wheel way too quickly and careen into the exit lane. I speed down the exit ramp and take a right toward a Stop & Shop. We come to a screeching halt, empty out of the car, and go running into the minimart. Not because I want beef jerky. Because I want out of this car.

As we enter, the doors bing, and I try to get my thoughts together. I think about my plan: *think it, do it.* I should just do anything that comes into my mind. Maybe that's the best way to figure out what this spirit wants. But I can't even get my thoughts straight and figure out what I'm feeling or wanting because my friends are going completely nuts. On the other hand, at least I got out of the car. One mission: accomplished.

"Here, here, here," Kate rips open a huge bag of jerky and shoves a piece in my mouth.

I spit it out. It's disgusting. It's not even food.

"No way," Jay says. "That's Teriyaki flavor, Kate. *No one* can be destined to eat Teriyaki flavor." He urgently points to the jerky shelf. "Get Original!"

This new flavor is no better. It leaves a thick salt layer on my tongue and that, combined with the panic and the mini-mart lighting—I feel like I might go down. My friends are no help; panic has stripped them of all rational thought. Not that I can blame them. As they whirl around me, I realize they've snapped into some sort of heist-movie mode, like we're a bunch of bandits pulling off the snack robbery of the century—which Kate actually is. Her pilfering tendencies have kicked in and she's stuffing all kinds of horrible meat sticks in her pockets and heading for the door. I grab her arm and make her pay the cashier. In a blur, we slam money down on the counter, and then we're running back to the Wagon like it's our trusty getaway van.

And then, the *truly* unexpected, Jay shoves a lit *cigarette* into my mouth.

"A cigarette?" I cough.

"I thought maybe that beef jerky could be a symbol for something else." He sounds embarrassed, as if uttering the words make them sound as moronic as they are—which is the only thing I'm sure of right now.

"You can't be serious," I croak.

But he's just staring at me, or staring at the spirit, I don't know which.

"OMG it's the END TIMES," Kate moans. "Jay has a fake ID."

"You *dawg*," Noah says in dry voice.

Jay shrugs. "Cousin has a really fancy printer."

I'm coughing—and coughing, and coughing. The cigarette is *horrible*. I throw it out the window.

"You guys," I say between hacks. "I don't think I'm supposed to *smoke*. I don't think we're getting this. Shouldn't spirits try to get us to do more important stuff than . . ." My voice trails off. Kate and Jay are frowning at me now.

"Dammit," Kate says. She deflates like a pool toy left out overnight. "I think it's gone. The spirit. I saw a flash of it, and now nothing. Do you feel anything?"

I shake my head no.

"Why doesn't it just *tell* us what Riley is supposed to do?" Jay asks. "Then we can get Riley to do it."

"That's not how discernment works," Noah says. "That was Ignatius's whole thing. They give us *sensations*. That's their only way to reach us. It could give Riley an idea to say something, to give us a clue. But she has to figure out what that is for herself."

I'm still softly hacking and silently apologizing to my lungs. "Can someone hand me a Vitamin Water?"

As the cold, sweet, vitamin-B infused liquid slides down my throat, I start to pull myself together. Now I'm not thinking about jerky or cigarettes or symbolism. All I'm thinking is that I want to know what I'm supposed to do.

I want to know how to help my mom.

Chapter 14

Information Ninjas

The front lobby of the CPL is intense. There's a crazy-huge entry with carpet that looks like it's covered in hundreds of giant rubies. And behind the front desk is this big carved wooden—*thing*. It almost looks like an organ? Or an altar? And the ceiling is domed and covered with gem-shaped blue and orange tiles. It feels like we've stepped into a giant jewelry box.

Jay confidently strides up to the front desk. "I need to see a librarian," he says, dropping his voice to a deeper tone, as if he's asking to meet with a foreign dignitary or something.

The woman behind the counter is totally cool. She looks like she's just out of college. She's wearing an old-school blouse with a peter pan collar, a tweed jacket, and super-huge black-rimmed glasses.

"Well that's a good thing," she says sarcastically, peering over her thick rims. "Because you're looking at one."

Jay smiles and looks all flustered for a second. He kind of leans on the front desk and gets closer. "Cool. We're sort of on a mission."

"We're doing research," I interrupt, nudging Jay out of the way. "On a Catholic saint. Saint Ignatius of Loyola."

"Oh?" she asks, raising her eyebrows. "For European history class?"

"Um, no," I say. "We're just . . . interested."

She lights up. I think I just learned my first research lesson. *Librarians: tell them you're interested in arcane subject matter best left for college.*

"Research just for the hell of it? That's so cool," she says. Then she pauses. She peers over her glasses at us. "But wait. Shouldn't you be in school right now?"

"We have this period and the next period free," Noah lies way too smoothly.

"Wow. And you're spending your free time here? That's awesome." She takes off her glasses and kind of waves her arms around as she keeps talking, like Noah does. I wonder if this is some sort of shared trait among the very smart: arm-waving in times of intellectual excitement. "We've actually had *a lot* of people come in asking about Ignatius and the Jesuits because of Pope Francis. He's the very first Jesuit pope in history, you know. And *Time's* Man of the Year. I mean, I'm totally against male-dominated church patriarchies, but even I have to admit, he's kind of a rock star. I mean, he goes around kissing female prisoners' feet and says we have to save the environment from becoming a pile of filth. *Winning.*"

Noah nudges my arm and whispers in my ear. "Isn't that redundant? Male-dominated patriarchies?"

"We're aware of Pope Francis," Kate interjects. "But we kind of have to get back to school soon. Can you tell us where to start?"

The librarian's arms flop to her sides. "Of course. History

Department. Sixth Floor. Louis Stokes wing. Ask for Gary once you get there. Good luck."

WHEN THE ELEVATOR OPENS on the sixth floor, a guy with a head full of perfect, black braids is waiting for us. He's wearing a red CPL shirt and jeans.

"I'm Gary," he says, motioning for us to follow him. "Liz already called up. Said you guys were *interested* in Saint Ignatius." He leads us to an empty table with a cool little green study lamp on it. "So what do you need to know? Are we talking basics here?"

"No. Not basics," Noah says, matching Gary's confidence. I can't help but notice how comfortable Noah seems as he sits in a plastic orange chair. It makes me happy; there really are places in the world that are safe for people like Noah, safe from idiotic bullies like Carl and the air band crew. "Two things, really . . . What languages Ignatius might have known, and the second: an extremely detailed history of Jesuit symbolism."

Gary nods. "Dig it." His eyes flicker slightly, as if Noah has passed some kind of CPL hipster test with flying colors. "Tell me what phase you're in," he says. "Still on secondary sources or have you moved on to primaries?"

"Huh?" Kate asks. She pulls a granola bar out of her backpack and starts chomping down.

"Um, can you eat that in the World Maps Café?" Gary asks loudly, with a frozen smile. Kate sighs and stuffs the bar back into her bag. "Thanks. We have a rodent problem. So . . . primary sources. What I mean is, have you read enough material already that you are now looking at what Ignatius and the early Jesuits actually wrote themselves?"

We all look at each other. I force myself to stay quiet and not say what I want to. *Let's see. Have we looked at actual documents? Like, say, the lost original manuscript of* The Spiritual Exercises *written by the Saint himself?*

"You could say primary sources," I respond in the silence. "Definitely primary."

Gary nods and motions for us to follow him. He takes us to a computer terminal and uses this as a teaching moment, settling into a very obviously well-rehearsed spiel. He shows us how to search the catalogue and digitally scroll through shelf contents. Then he escorts us back into the elevator, down into the bowels of the library, and through darkened rows of books. We watch in awe as Gary reads the numbers on book spines like they're tea leaves. He's amazing, really. It's like watching an artist at work in his studio.

"Bingo," he says as his fingers come to a stop mid-row. "An early translation of Ignatius. Translations often have prefaces that discuss the various languages of prior versions. And as for symbolism . . ." He breaks off and jogs to a computer console. We watch as he returns with a slip of paper. He points us in the direction of the Fine Arts section, and holds out a list of call numbers for books about early Jesuit art.

Jay takes it and shoves it into his pocket. "Thanks, Gary," he says. "You were a huge help, man. I mean it."

"No worries," he says, heading back to the elevator.

When the doors close behind him, a familiar idea comes: *Think it, do it.*

I look at Kate and Noah. "Jay and I will go," I blurt out. "To find the art books."

Kate raises her eyebrows. "Okaaay," she says. "I guess Noah and I will stay here and read what we've got. You two . . . have fun."

I roll my eyes at her and grab Jay's arm. We head for the elevators. I push the button, anxiously looking at fellow library patrons as they pass. I'm fully aware of how on edge I am, how I expect to see Mom around every corner. I jump a little as the elevator bell chimes upon arrival. The doors swoosh open. No one is inside. We go in and stand in the elevator alone. I glance over at him as the car starts to move. *It's time. I've liked him long enough.*

It's an urge, it's a whim—could be coming from me, could be coming from a spirit who's messing with me. Who knows? Maybe I'm wrong. Or maybe this is what spirits have been trying to get me to do since the ninth grade. I've got to figure out what they want; maybe they want this.

Jay looks at the floor, lost in thought. Or maybe sadness.

"You okay?" I ask. I'm wishing he'd look at me; I want to know if he sees a spirit. But he doesn't. He keeps his eyes firmly on the elevator floor.

"Yeah," he says. "I guess."

The thought again: *do it.*

I take what I hope is a non-obvious little side-step closer to him, catch a whiff of the drier sheet scent that's coming from his shirt. I plot my course. I've never done this before. I go over what I imagine the steps should be: *lean, turn, lip alignment, contact, done.* Right? And if there's a spirit with me, urging me on, I need to move quickly. It would be so weird for Jay to be kissed by me—when he doesn't see just me. It needs to be over before he has time to realize what's happening.

I take a deep breath. But before I can whip up the nanosecond of heroics that the lip-alignment step requires, the elevator lurches to a halt with a loud chime. We're at the Fine Arts floor. The doors slide open, and like a deflating balloon, all the romantic tension that may or may not have been building in the elevator empties out in one sad whoosh of air.

"I need a minute," Jay says as we step out. He hands me the list of call numbers. "Can you find the books? I'm going to head outside. Okay?"

"Um," I say slowly. "Okay." If it weren't so amazingly obvious that he wanted to be alone, I would try to go with him. But the armor of numbness fits better than ever. I play it cool. And he takes off.

I FIND A FEW books on Jesuit symbolism and head back to the History Section. Jay is nowhere in sight. Kate has spread a variety of snacks out on the table with the cool green study lamp, and Noah is hunched over three different books.

"You're going to get us kicked out," I say, eyeing Kate's snack selection. "You're only supposed to eat in the maps café."

"Whatever," she says, popping a handful of gummy bears into her mouth. "I find breaking small rules strangely fulfilling."

Noah pats the seat next to him. "Sit down. Check out what I found in the book Gary gave us."

I do and he scoots our chairs close. He holds up a green book so I can see the front. *The Spiritual Exercises.* "This is the oldest English translation of Ignatius's book that they have here. Published in 1914." He sets it down and opens to the preface. "Here it talks about all the versions that ever existed. Basically, there was the original that Saint Ignatius wrote by hand, which is lost." His eyes sparkle. "Which is I'm sure what you guys found in the cave. And it's likely a mix of three languages: totally incorrect Old Castilian, made-up Latin words, and Ignatius's native Basque."

"Made-up Latin?" I ask.

Noah nods. Then I remember when Jay read some of the history of the saint. How in early life he was terrible at Latin and didn't know it very well. "And what's Old Castilian?"

"Don't know," Noah says. "Kate, can you Google?"

"On it," she says. She takes a swig of Mountain Dew and pops more gummy bears in her mouth. "Okay, Castilian in Ignatius's time would be Old Castilian, or Medieval Spanish. It's just an old form of Spanish that was used from the tenth century through the fifteenth."

"So that's why some of the words in the original look *sort of* Spanish," I say.

Noah nods. "So maybe the words in the original manuscript that totally stumped Google Translate are—"

"Made-up Latin," I conclude. "Since he made them up, Google Translate couldn't make sense of them at all. So it threw up its little digital hands and guessed Finnish. And Slovak. But Ignatius got some of the Latin and Castilian close enough, that GT was able to detect them."

Noah smiles and kicks back in his chair. "Think we could have future careers in the FBI? CIA?"

The elevator chimes, and Jay emerges. He slides into the open chair at our table. We all scowl at exactly the same moment. In his wake is an unmistakable, completely nasty, almost choking cloud of cigarette smoke.

"OMG," Kate says, pulling her T-shirt up over her mouth. "You *reek*."

"What?" Jay asks, trying to look all innocent.

"*Really?*" Noah says. It's all any of us need to say.

Jay runs a hand through his bed-head hair. "Don't judge, okay? I kept the smokes I bought at the gas station on our way up here. I just . . . needed one."

"What do you mean, you *needed* one?" I ask. "What does that even mean?" But before I can continue my smoking inquisition, I see something. Where Jay sits. A shadow passing over him: flashes of someone I've seen before; I recognize the mean hazel eyes and blond hair. It's the same person I saw when this was all starting, when Jay was texting Sarah that night after we got back from the cemetery.

Kate scoots her chair back from the table. Her eyes are wide and glossed over like they're coated with gummy bear sugar. I know she sees it, too. She stares at the spirit flickering inside Jay, and then holds her hand over her mouth like she's going to throw up.

"*I can't take this anymore,*" she whispers. And then she makes a beeline for the bathroom.

Noah watches Kate go and then leans toward me. "Is he—?"

I nod my head and mouth the word *yes,* not saying it out loud. And as I sit there watching it happen, thinking back to the elevator before Jay took off to smoke, something occurs to me. I wonder if he was inhabited before he went outside, and if this spirit we're seeing is an evil one. Maybe he was with Jay in the elevator, and I missed it because I wasn't looking at him. And as I inhale the third-hand smoke emanating from Jay's clothes and I see the sad, lost-rebel look in his eyes, I wonder if damaged people are easy targets. Because I know that beside the definition of *damaged* in the dictionary, there needs to be a hyperlink to Jay's Facebook page and to mine. And to our whole Back on Track crew. I wonder how often evil spirits have been toying with all of us—the messed up, the grieving—subtly steering us in the wrong direction.

The spirit passes, and Jay is back to himself.

I look down at the pile of books we've amassed on the table, and the memory of Mom's last night alive comes to me again. How there might have been evil spirits there, urging me to stay quiet. How I ignored the good ones crying out to stop her. And I know I've got to figure this out, how to discern what these spirits want from us—and fast. I don't ever want to make another mistake like I did that night. And if there's a way to see Mom again, to tell her I'm sorry, to help her, I have to figure it out. I *have* to.

"Hand me Kate's Mountain Dew," I say to Noah. "I'm going to need it."

Chapter 15

Read the Signs.

I haven't even been reading for fifteen minutes when the text comes in from Dad:

WHY ARE YOU NOT AT SCHOOL?

Oh, no. We have bungled the skipping school protocol. Kate must have gotten distracted and not set her phone alarm after all. Not that I can blame her. Despite my earlier request that someone set an alarm so we would all remember to text home before second period started, apparently, no one did. And my dad's direction is clear and still in all caps:

GET TO SCHOOL. NOW.

I was hoping I'd get some leeway, given that I witnessed Dad getting to second base on the front porch last night, but apparently my payback for that has run out.

AFTER A TORTUOUS CHECK-IN with the front office, we receive our usual sentence of lunch detention for the next three days. Then we are dismissed. I slide into my seat near the end of third period Biology.

And immediately, I start freaking out. I can't stop looking for my mom and for other spirits in the people around me. I awkwardly glance at everyone in the lab; I even stare into the reflection of my dark iPhone screen to see if I can catch a flicker in my own eyes. I notice a thin sheen of sweat forming on my brow. More disturbingly, I feel it on my back as I squirm against the seat back. Which is extremely gross.

After Bio, I head for the snack machine in the cafeteria, thinking that a candy bar may calm my nerves. I fish for a dollar, smooth it between my hands, and reach up to feed it into the machine. But before I can get the bill in place, douche bag Carl cuts in front of me. He's wearing a super-expensive brand-name shirt that has sailboats on it. Because his family, the elite of the Cleveland burbs, does *so much sailing* on Lake Erie, they feel the need to broadcast it.

I'm not the least bit surprised when he nudges me out of the way, feeds his own dollar into the machine, and gets the very last Snickers. Nor am I surprised when he looks at me, shrugs, and flashes his usual shitty grin.

I'm not even terribly surprised at what happens next. Just extremely terrified and disturbed.

As he smiles, I see a spirit. A girl. She flickers in and out with a smirk on her face just as evil looking as his. I see glimpses of her long black dress and a tiny pillbox hat on her head, a black feather jutting out. And as he walks away, she flashes once more. Then she's gone.

I think back to all the times spirits have probably been around me, especially with ass-hats like Carl, and I just didn't realize it. Like the day Carl came down out of the tree and knocked Noah's Coke out of his hands: evil spirit. None of us saw him do it, but I'd bet anything that's what happened. And the night Jay was epically lame and texted Sarah back after we got home from the cemetery: evil spirit. Maybe an evil spirit even got Kate to want to join air band in the first place. Or buy things with her mom's credit card. Maybe evil spirits point Jay toward the wrong girls all the time. Maybe his picker isn't broken. Maybe he just can't tell a good spirit from a bad one.

I hurry down the hall. "I'm not okay," I say to Kate as she stuffs books into her locker.

"I'm going to need more details," she responds, slamming her locker shut and spinning the combination lock. "Is it the whole seeing-spirits thing? Or something else I'm not aware of?"

I give her a small smile, and she puts her arm around my shoulders. She leans on me as we make our way toward the cafeteria. I feel wobbly, world-weary. And I'm pretty sure I'm too young to feel this way.

"We'll figure this out," she says. She tries but fails to sound sure of herself. Then she looks me straight in the eye. "We *will*."

But I know she catches the expression on my face and realizes she's not helping. Because there's no way she knows what she's talking about. I may never see my mom again. I'll see spirits for sure, but maybe not my mom. Ever. And just guessing that I will is making it way worse. We turn the corner and head into the cafeteria. She tries again.

"*Struggling montage*, Riley. That's what this is. We're just not at the happy ending, that's all." She chews her fingernails as we walk toward the pile of cafeteria trays. I glance at her hands. The nails are nubs; she's picked at her cuticles until they're bloody. It's not lost on me that she's putting so much effort into appearing okay for my benefit, to keep it together, hoping her outsides will help my insides.

"You're right," I say. "It's the struggling montage. Totally struggling montage."

She picks up a cafeteria tray and gets in line. I follow. Instead of focusing on my uninspiring lunch choices, I start doing the staring thing again. I look at the cafeteria ladies, all the people in line, the cooks in the back. I scan the cafeteria, looking at all the groups, at all the stray students lingering at the sides of the room. I see Jay at a table and wave. Then I go back to searching. Over and over. Searching for my mom.

"Um, are you okay to eat lunch with Jay?" I ask. "Without me?"

"Yeah, I guess? If you are?"

"I just need to be alone for a little bit. The cafeteria, with all these people—"

"I get it," she says. "Go."

I STOP BY MY locker, grab my bag, and head to the auditorium. Air band practice will not be in session; there won't be any popular girls on stage doing dance moves. I push open the swinging doors and see the seats unoccupied, the stage vacant. The floor is strewn with empty Gatorade cups and candy wrappers. Just as I hoped, no one's here.

I walk up the stairs to the stage and sit on the edge, dangling my feet over the gym floor below. I unzip my bag, pull out the original manuscript and open it. I run my hand over the wrinkled Magis section.

Nos omnostria sumus . . .

I look below those words and see the symbol, the series of squiggly, unconnected lines. I think back to what we learned at the CPL, that Ignatius likely used some incorrect or made-up Latin in his original text because he didn't know it all that well at first. I reach for my cell phone and instead of Google

Translate, I pull up an online Latin dictionary. And instead of entering the whole phrase—which totally stumped GT earlier—I enter just the first three letters of *omnostria*: *o, m,* and *n*. If Ignatius made this word up and was trying his best at Latin, then maybe he got the root of the word right at least?

Sure enough, I get two options for Latin words that begin with *o, m,* and *n*. There's *omnis* and *omnes*. And they are different forms of a word that means: *all; the whole; each and every one.*

Next, I enter *nos*.

That one comes up right away. We should have entered it alone the first time we looked. Its Latin meaning is clear: *we*.

I put the two together. We and all. *We* and *all*. Ignatius must have meant *Nos omnes sumus*. I enter all three and get *WE ARE ALL*. But *we are all* what? We are all . . . squiggly lines.

Perfect. In a way: true. We are all a mishmash of indecipherable crap. That is a spiritual philosophy I can relate to.

But I know it means more than that. I sigh and pull out one of the library books on Jesuit symbols. I flip through the pages looking for something—anything—that resembles the squiggly-lined symbol in the manuscript. But all I find is the seal for the Jesuit Society. It's become extremely familiar. I saw it last night when I was Googling Jesuit symbols with Noah at my house. There's a cross, the letters I.H.S., and then three nails below it in a *V* shape. And the whole thing is surrounded by rays of sun. The book says that the *I, H,* and *S* are supposed to be the Greek letters—iota, eta, and sigma. Which are the first three letters of a name: Jesus, in Greek.

I stop reading. I don't need to read the next part about the three nails in a *V* shape below; I'm pretty sure I know what those mean. You don't have to be a religious expert to know that Jesus was crucified—with nails. So the Jesuit seal has an abbreviation for the word Jesus and some nails on it. Which tells me exactly nothing.

Just then I hear a noise. I look up. It's Judy, one of our school janitors, coming through the auditorium doors in the back with a ginormous dust mop. I wave and she waves back. She goes to work on the mess the air band kids have left behind. I listen to the soft swooshing of her broom and the tumbling of paper Gatorade cups as they're swept along the floor, and it sounds so sad to me. They should've cleaned the mess up themselves.

I watch her at the back of the gym as she methodically sweeps up the air band detritus. I follow her every move, hoping that maybe any minute she'll kind of drift up the aisle all ghost-like and stop right in front of me with her broom. That she'll flicker in and out—and in her place, I'll see Mom.

But she doesn't. She just keeps sweeping. There are no spirits here, apparently.

I get up and search in the wings, looking for a roll of plastic garbage bags or a big rolling bin so I can help Judy with the mess. As I open cabinets and a closet in the back, I let myself imagine seeing mom again.

It occurs to me that all I've ever thought about is what I would say to her if I ever got the chance, but now a different question hits me. *What will she say to me?* Will she yell about that last night I saw her alive? Will she ask how I could have been so heartless—to tell her I hated her, to let her get behind the wheel of a car, to just let it all happen and do nothing to stop it? Will she ask how I could've been so clueless? How I could've missed the spirit that was trying to help me, to help her? Will she finally say what I *know* is the truth, that she regrets ever having a child, that the day of my birth was the worst day of her life? How being a mom is actually a really crappy job, lots of hard work, lots of sacrifice, lots to lose? Does she wish someone had told her it *so* wasn't worth it?

And what will I say back? That I know.

I'm sorry, I'm sorry, I'm sorry.

And I am.

All at once, I hear Judy cry out. I run back onto the stage, and Judy is just in front of it, pointing to the floor. I look down, and in the pile of garbage she's swept from underneath the front row of seats is a mouse—a dead one. It's all curled up, its hands knotted in tiny fists, its long tail stiff and lifeless.

"I hate it when I find these," Judy says. "And I still squeal every time." She wipes the sweat away from her forehead. Then she laughs a little.

But I don't. Because I feel like it's a sign. An omen telling me that I'll never figure this out. That I'll die before I lay eyes on my mother again. That I'll run around my life like a mouse trapped in a school auditorium. Always searching for the way out.

Judy says something else, but I don't pay attention. Because I get a text. From Noah.

I bailed on school again.

Meet me after. Think I found something.

WHAT IS IT?

I don't think the nails are nails. Get it?

NO.

I run down the stage steps, typing as I go.

But I'm on my way.

I GRAB KATE AND Jay and we leave school, knowing this will be the death knell for the rest of junior year. We'll probably get lunch detention for the remainder of our days and face grueling sentences from our parents. Well, everyone but Jay will get in trouble at home. His mom probably won't even answer the phone when the school calls.

I wonder if that's what will happen to my dad now that Sammy's in the picture. If he'll become a shadow of the person who used to be the central human being in my life. I push the thought away.

We drive to Noah's and when we get there, we don't bother texting him to open the door. We've been through this before. We head straight for the garage door keypad and type in the dorkiest garage code in all the world: 3.141. Pi to three decimal places. Noah's parents are at work. He's in his room, which is still strewn with research and books and half-full coffee mugs, hunched over his desk. He doesn't even look up as we arrive. Kate flops stomach first onto his bed and bites at her already-destroyed nails.

"Tell me you've figured out a way to make this stop," she says. "I can't stand to see spirits anymore. Like maybe we need to start wearing garlic necklaces?"

Jay sits on the floor next to a pile of books. I join him. Noah does, too. "So what did you find?" I say to Noah. "Nails aren't nails?"

"Maybe we could just *destroy* it," Kate says, maybe to herself. She kicks her legs onto the wall behind Noah's bed, creating a perfect *L* shape with her body. "Like we were going to before." Then she tilts her legs away from the wall and starts doing air bicycle. "We could take the necklace into shop class and cut it to bits with the metal saw. Or we could melt it! With a blowtorch."

This suggestion makes me more than a little nervous. The last time Kate and Jay suggested destroying the cross, Noah took off.

"No," I say. "Not a good idea."

Without realizing it, I've been tugging at the threads of Noah's bedroom carpet beside me. I've created a little pile of cream-colored fuzz, and there's a growing bald spot on the floor. If Noah has noticed, he keeps it to himself.

"Not that this experience has made me super religious or anything," Jay says. "But I'm not on board with destroying the necklace anymore. First of all, it's still my dad's. And second, I don't think I want *destroying a crucifix* on my life's résumé. I mean, that can't be good, right?"

"There's no Jesus on it," Noah pipes up. "So it's technically not a crucifix. Just a cross—"

"OMG what does 'nails aren't nails' mean?" I nearly shout.

"Sorry," he says. He shoves a book my way. It's another book on Jesuit symbolism we checked out from the CPL, and he's got the page open to a drawing of the Jesuit Society's seal. "See the nails below the letters I.H.S.? How they're in a *V* shape?"

"Um, guys?" Kate says, dropping her head over the edge of the bed, looking at us upside down. "We don't need a book to explain the nails. Jesus was crucified. *With nails.*"

"But what if they aren't just nails?" Noah says. "What if they aren't in a *V* shape? What if they are meant to actually stand for the letter *V*?"

I pull an elastic band off my wrist and whip my hair into a knot on top of my head. "Which would mean the Jesuit seal doesn't read I.H.S. It reads I.H.S.V.?"

"Exactly," Noah says. "Google it. You'll see what I mean."

Jay jumps on it first. He pulls out his cell phone and reads what comes up, the glowing screen lighting his face. "I get a definition from an acronyms site. It says I.H.S.V. stands for *In Hoc Signo Vinces*. Which is Latin: *In this sign, conquer.*"

"Get it?" Noah asks, his blue eyes shining. We stare at him blankly. "It's a *clue*. Somehow this sign, the seal for the Jesuit Society, will allow us to solve Ignatius's secret. *With this sign*, we'll *conquer* the secret in his book. Get it? I think this seal holds the key."

"Wait," Kate says with her head still hanging over the bed. "Is that it? That's all you've figured out? That we need this Jesuit seal somehow?" All the blood is running into her face and gravity is forcing her mouth into a creepy upside-down smile. "And did I *seriously* just bail on school twice in one day, risking groundation for life, for *that*?"

"Yeah, I don't know that this really means anything," Jay says, still staring at his phone. He begins to scroll. "This says that I.H.S.V. is a reference to Constantine. To the Christianization of Rome. Maybe that's all it's referring to. Like, how the Christian sign was taking over." He tosses his phone onto the carpet next to him, like it's a mini-librarian who just let him down.

I ignore them all and pull Noah's book into my lap. I study the drawing of the Jesuit seal.

Silently, I beg: *Tell me what you know.*

I focus on each part of it, slowly dissecting it in my mind. It's decorated with rays of sunshine that emanate from the circular center. There's a straight ray and then a squiggly one. A straight one, and then a squiggly one. All around the seal. It makes me think of the squiggly, unconnected lines in Ignatius's manuscript—but that doesn't help. I open my backpack and pull out the original manuscript and turn to the Magis section.

Jay peeks over my shoulder. "Seriously, it just looks like chicken scratch," he says, pointing to Ignatius's squiggly lines. "Maybe it's not even a symbol to begin with."

I swivel and turn my back to him. "You can be a real downer, you know that? Now let me think in peace."

He gets up and flops on the bed next to Kate. I can't help but notice he reeks of cigarette smoke again.

I go back to the Jesuit seal. "In this sign," I whisper to myself. "In this sign."

I keep running my eyes over it, piece by piece. *Letters: I.H.S. And nails in a* V *shape below. I.H.S.V. In this sign, conquer. And a cross above the letter* H.

But then I stop. And realize I'm wrong. The cross is not *above* the letter *H: it's on top of it.* The end of the cross *intersects* the H; the cross and the letter are *put together.*

"You guys," I say. I wave my arms in the air, all excited, hipster-librarian-resident-genius style, which I never do. Then I jab a finger at the seal. "See how the cross is *touching* the letter *H?* How they're *put together?* And just like Jay said, the squiggly lines in Ignatius's manuscript look like chicken scratch. Right?"

They all look at me like I'm speaking one of the totally incomprehensible foreign languages that Google Translate has offered us in the past few days, like Basque, or Finnish, or Slovak.

"Chicken scratch. *Scratches,*" I say. "That's what made me think of it. What's on the back of Ignatius's cross necklace?"

"We already know it's the Latin word *magis*," Jay says. "Which means more. Which was just a clue that there was more to Ignatius's theories."

"Right," I say. "But what *else* was on the back of the cross?"

"OMG," Kate says. She gets off the bed and does rapid fire mini-jumps of excitement in the middle of the room. "OMG. I get it."

"Um, can you two code-cracking wizards fill us in?" Noah asks, with maybe just a touch of envy, which is oddly endearing.

"The back of the cross," Kate says, still jumping. Her black hair flops around her shoulders as she bounces. "It's all scratched up!" Then she stands still and leans her face close to Noah. And ruffles his hair. "But maybe they aren't scratches," she says with a know-it-all smile.

Noah looks at me, confused.

"What she means is that maybe the scratches on the cross are a series of unconnected lines," I explain. "Just like the lines in the manuscript. And the Jesuit seal is telling us to put the cross together with the squiggly lines in the manuscript . . ." I wait for it to dawn on Noah and Jay. Noah gets it first, and his NASA blues flare like we're well into a rocket launch countdown.

"And the scratches on the back of the cross and the squiggly lines in the manuscript will *match*," he says. "The Jesuit Society's seal is telling us to put the cross together with the symbol in the manuscript. Maybe they'll spell a word. And if we do that—"

"We'll conquer," Jay finishes, as it dawns on him, too.

Hope rises in my chest like a balloon, pressing against the back of my ribcage. "And we'll know what the spirits are doing," I say softly. "We'll know what my mother was doing with that living woman in the store. We'll know if she needs help."

Kate resumes doing mini-jumps in celebration. She grabs Jay's hand and tries to get him to join. But he doesn't. Instead, he holds his hand out to Noah.

"Hand it over, bro," he says. "You've had the cross long enough. We need it back now. To solve this."

The launch-countdown excitement fades from Noah's eyes. He looks at Kate, then at Jay. And then at me. Then his eyes drop.

"I don't have it," he confesses.

I don't have to respond. The searing, hawk-eye look I give to Noah says it loud and clear: *Then tell us where it is.*

"I can try to get it back," he says. He gets up and gets his wallet off his dresser, and then starts searching for his car keys. "No promises, but I'll try. But you can't come with me. I can't tell you where it is. Just . . . wait for me at Jay's house."

Jay shakes his head, his jaw tight, but he nods. And if he can agree, so can I. Kate nods, too. Of course, we all look at each other behind Noah's back. And this look, too, is clear as a bell: *We let him go. But we follow him. We absolutely and totally FOLLOW HIM.*

Chapter 16

Get It Back.

My car is a pretty difficult thing to miss, what with its stop-sign coloring and sexy, wagon-esque profile. There's no way we can follow Noah in it without being caught.

At least that's the argument we use to justify stealing Noah's dad's "fancy car." It's a white Chevy Camaro that he drives only on weekends and prizes, at times, above Noah. We figure that, for this mission, it has two things going for it. 1) It's a weekday, so Noah will assume that it's not his father's Camaro. (Camaros have invaded Ohio like some sort of invasive insect species. They crawl over the highways in hordes, so we won't stand out.) And 2) He never in a million years would even *think* we'd have the moxie to steal his father's car.

Jay and Kate volunteer me as the most trusted driver, and they have a point.

So off we go in a stolen vehicle, our own real-life version of Grand Theft Auto. I try to hang back as much as I can, with at least three cars between us, as I follow Noah's Honda onto I-77 North.

As the trip stretches on, I really hope he's not taking us out of state. Kate squirms for all of us in the backseat as we pass exit after exit. We don't listen to music. We don't talk. Finally, north of Brecksville, Jay suggests a game.

"Test of Wills?" He looks over at me from the passenger seat and raises an eyebrow.

"And that would be?" I take my eyes off the road for just a second and glance at him. He looks giddy. He proceeds to turn on the heat in the car. In May.

"We roll the windows up and crank the heat as high as it will go," he says. "Whoever cracks first loses."

"No," Kate says, leaning up front. "Just, no. We are *not* doing that. We are not messing with a stolen car. What if we break the heater somehow? Plus, I already have claustrophobia in this tiny tin can as it is. When I crack in the game, it will be cracking by vomiting."

"Yeah," I say, gripping the wheel. I pass an enormous truck on the right and remind myself that my most immediate life goal should be to avoid not only a wreck but also any scratch that would indicate it even left the garage. "That's a negative on Test of Wills, dude. Sounds horrible."

"Fine," Jay says, turning the AC back on. "But don't ever say I didn't try to get you to have fun."

Kate ignores Jay by typing something into her phone, and I ignore him by focusing on Noah's Honda, which is now about ten cars ahead. It's relatively easy to stay undetected on the interstate, but it gets harder when Noah takes an exit onto Harvard Avenue and drives east. Then he turns onto a more rural road I've never even heard of: 10,000 Miles Avenue.

We pass vast expanses of empty fields. I wonder where on earth Noah could be going. But I don't have to question for long. We pass through an unmarked wrought iron gate, and once we do, the green fields are no longer empty. They're filled with miles and miles of headstones.

Why did I not expect this?

It's the biggest cemetery I've ever seen. Sprinkled among the graves are tall mausoleums, all dirty-white marble with carved angels and doves and statues of Jesus holding up one hand like he's waving goodbye. I see flat headstones like my mom's, others cracked and standing crooked like rows of broken iPhones.

Maybe half a mile in, we pass a huge white wooden sign: CALVARY CEMETERY. And beneath that, in smaller letters: CATHOLIC CEMETERIES ASSOCIATION.

I slow down, dropping far behind Noah, losing sight of him over rolling hills that seem to never end. I don't want him to glimpse us in his rearview; ours (his father's) is the only other car on this road. We pass gravesite after gravesite, little flowering trees, a pond, and a fountain. It seems wrong that you can drive right through a cemetery. I feel like I'm gunning a convertible through the middle of a church or a hospital. I mean: you have to take your shoes off when you go in most people's houses, but it's okay to drive right through their final resting places?

In the distance, at the top of a tall hill, I spot a building that looks like a funeral home. That's where Noah is headed. It's one story and L-shaped, with a domed roof over the middle. And right beside the parking lot is this statue of Jesus. He's standing on what looks like a giant stone exercise ball, and he's holding both hands up to the sky. I'm not sure it's a very reassuring pose; I'm questioning the artist's choices. Something about Jesus balancing on a ball is disconcerting, and the look on his face is, well, kind of *anguished.* Or worried, at the very least. To me, he should be looking super chill and confident, like, *Hey, families who just buried someone: Don't worry. I GOT THIS.*

Noah parks his car in front, gets out, and disappears inside.

Only when there's no chance he'll spot us do I park the car on the side of the road beside a tree. I get my bag out of the back, and we all make our way up the hill to the building. Kate and I tiptoe up to one of the windows and peek in, to see if we can catch a glimpse of Noah. But it's too dark inside to see much.

Jay gently opens the front door, sticks his head in and motions for us to follow.

It's not quite as dim inside as it seemed from the window. Late afternoon sunlight blinks through leaves that cover the skylights above. Jay takes off to look for Noah in the side rooms, while Kate and I stay in the main atrium. There's an altar at the front. I look around and notice the walls are covered with big squares of marble. Little bunches of fake flowers jut out of each one like perky prom corsages. Kate and I walk a bit closer. Etched into the marble squares are names. And dates. Of birth and death.

"Dude," Kate whispers, grasping my arm. "Are there, like, dead people in the *walls?*"

"Looks like it," I whisper back.

"I'm out. Can't. Cope." And she slips out the backdoor of the chapel and into the bright sunshine behind the building.

"Noah?" Jay calls as he comes back into the atrium. "Come out, man. We're here."

Silence.

He sighs and sits down in a pew. "I don't get it. Why would he come here? Cam isn't buried here. And where did he go?"

Kate pops her head back in the door. "You guys," she hisses.

"There's a little house out back. Down the hill. You can't see it from the road. And it looks like someone lives in it."

We follow her outside. She's right. On the slope behind the chapel, maybe a hundred yards away, stands a little white house. There's a garden full of dying tomatoes, a porch swing by the front door, and a Dodge Durango sitting in the driveway. At first, the house looks normal enough, but the longer I stand there, the creepier it seems. It's like a faded photograph, worn around the edges. Chunks of paint are peeling off the wooden siding and several roof shingles are ajar, tilted toward the sky like crooked teeth. Its green shutters are warped and the windowpanes must be the original glass—thick and wavy like old fashioned Coke bottles.

"You think Noah . . . went in there?" Kate asks.

"It's worth a try," Jay says.

As we walk toward the house, I squint at the windows, trying to see if there's any movement inside. There isn't.

We get close enough to see a heavy iron door knocker on the front door. It's in the shape of an angel, but he looks like an angry angel. Or at least a miserable angel. There's a window on the side of the house by the garden, so we crouch down and make our way toward it. Slowly, we stand up and peek in.

I draw in a sharp breath.

There's Noah. He's sitting in a wingback chair, talking to one of the most disheveled, pathetic-looking men I've ever seen. He looks homeless, but I'm guessing this is his home. His dark hair hangs down to his shoulders, matted and speckled with gray, and it's twisting in every direction. His beard is no better, kind of smashed in on one side and bushy on the other. Food stains are splattered down his white T-shirt and his blue jeans are full of holes.

My eyes drift across the room. Junk and tchotchkes are strewn everywhere; half-empty liquor bottles sit on every available flat surface. Underneath all the chaos, though, I spot some really pretty pieces. There's a giant grandfather clock ticking away in the corner; I can hear it, muffled but strong, through the glass. And beside that there's a beautiful piano piled high with dirty dishes and two broken lamps.

The man is talking, and his voice is getting louder and louder. Noah responds, but I can't understand what he says. The man looks unhappy about whatever it is. His voice starts to boom, his beard trembling as he yells. Finally, he gets up and storms out of the room.

Noah follows.

We run to the front door and start pounding like mad. I bang the angry angel door knocker, and Kate and Jay use their fists. We hear more yelling inside. I lean against the window beside the front door and press my ear to the glass. I can only catch bits and pieces of what the man is yelling.

"Not one more thing," he booms. Then something about the Bible. Adam and Eve. The apple. The words *knowledge*, and *ruins*, and *us*.

"What do we do?" Kate asks. "Break in? Call the cops?"

I keep silent rather than saying: *If we call the cops, we're the ones who will get arrested for trespassing and driving a stolen car.* I press my ear back to the glass. I hear something about a dogwood tree. A drainage pipe. Then a door slams.

"I'll try to find a way in," Jay says. He takes off down the porch steps and disappears around the side of the house. Inside, the voices go quiet. Kate bangs again with the angel knocker. No one answers.

But Jay appears around the corner, waving at us to follow him.

There's another steep hill behind the house. And Noah is at the top of it.

Heading away from us. With a shovel.

QUIETLY, WE FOLLOW. HE makes his way down the other side of the hill and stops at a pond that's ringed with dogwood trees. Sticking out in the middle of the water, past cattails and the sludgy banks, is a corrugated drainage pipe. Noah squints into the sunlight and appears to be counting trees.

"Dogwoods," Jay whispers. "You guys know the legend?"

"Please don't—" Kate starts.

"The blossoms. They have four white petals and each has a little blot of red at the end. Legend is that Jesus's cross was made of dogwood bark. So the tree was cursed and forever carries drops of his blood."

I look at the dogwoods. *So you have secrets, too?*

"*Shhh,*" Kate hisses. "Look."

Noah walks to the third tree to the right of the drainage pipe and inspects the trunk and the dirt around it. Then he plunges his shovel into the ground.

I take off running before I'm even aware of what I'm doing. Jay and Kate call me back, but I don't listen. I sprint as fast as I can toward Noah. And when I reach him, breathless, I drop my bag off my shoulder and hit my knees. I start digging with my hands. Because I know what he's trying to find in the dirt: the cross that will lead me back to my mom.

"Riley," Noah says. He kneels down beside me. "You shouldn't be here." He looks back in the direction of the house. His lips turn downward when he spots Jay and Kate at the top of the hill.

"You really thought we wouldn't follow you?" I ask.

"But I promised him I wouldn't tell anyone—"

"Just keep digging."

He shakes his head but acquiesces. And after what feels like ages, his shovel hits something. He tosses it aside and we both go at the hole with our hands. I see a glint of dirt-covered silver as Noah unearths the necklace. He holds it up in the dappled sunlight coming through the dogwood branches.

"He didn't even put it in a box or anything," Noah says slowly as the necklace gently sways in front of him. "I gave it to him for safekeeping. He was a prof on the team with Jay's dad. He helped find it. So it seemed right to give it back to him."

But I'm not listening to Noah. Not really.

Instead, I'm staring at the muddy cross and thinking one thing only:

Tell us your secret.

JAY AND KATE REACH us, and I pull the manuscript out of my bag. I'm afraid, but I'm not about to stop.

Wherever my mother went after we buried her six feet under, whatever it is she's doing with the living, whatever it is she wants . . . I need to know.

We huddle in the grass as I flip through the pages.

"Here it is." I point to the series of unconnected lines in the Magis section. Noah lays the cross on the page next to it. Just looking at them, they don't seem to match.

"I need a pen and someone's hand," I say. But no one has a pen. "Then somebody open a drawing app so I can sketch these two things together."

Kate gets her phone and opens her art app, which gives us a blank screen. With my finger, I carefully draw the scratches from the cross and the lines from the book on the same screen. And they *do* match. They make letters.

"The first word is—P-O-R-T-A-E. Maybe? Somebody pull up GT." I rub my finger over the cross, making sure I've gotten all the dirt off, copied every etched line. "And if that doesn't work, try a Latin dictionary."

"On it," Noah says, pulling his phone out of his back pocket.

I keep going. "I'm thinking the next letters are A-D and then C-A-E-L-U-M? Does that mean anything?"

"*Portae ad caelum,*" Noah says slowly. He types in the words. "And the words before the symbol are—"

"*Nos omnes sumus,*" I say. "I got that earlier from a Latin dictionary. He wrote *omnostria,* but I think he was going for *omnes.* Because he sucked at Latin when he wrote this."

"So the whole sentence is *nos omnes sumus portae ad caelum,*" Noah says as he taps away again at his cell screen. As I wait, I feel like angry hummingbirds have swarmed my stomach. They flutter madly, pecking at my insides.

"Does it mean anything?"

Noah looks at me. A breeze tickles my skin. "Yes."

The cemetery, the pond—it all feels unsettled around me, like I'm a dogwood branch being lifted by the wind. I try to calm down and pay attention to the twitter of a few distant birds and to my own breath. In and out, in and out.

"What is it?" Kate says, kneeling beside me now.

"I think it means . . ." Noah stops. He looks away, and I can see his thoughts coming together like he's gluing down the last piece of some elaborate model rocket. He looks in my eyes, checking to see if I'm ready. I nod. "I think it means that there's only one way to heaven. And it's through *you.*"

"What?" I put the book down on the damp soil. Scoot back. "*Me?* That makes no sense, I—"

"No," Noah says gently. "The pronoun form that Saint Ignatius uses is *nos*—which means *we*. All of us. Everyone. *Portae ad caelum*: doorways to heaven. We're all doorways. To the other side. That's what the dead are trying to do. To cross *through us*. The living. That's why they mess with us and try to influence us. That's why it's so important to discern what they want. Because if they get us to do something we're meant to do, then . . ."

I can't hear him anymore because the swarm of hummingbirds has left my stomach. Now they're all around me, enveloping me, swooping around my head. And I feel like I'm trying to catch them all with my hands, but they're slipping through, their green feathers slick and shiny. "So in the store, I saw my mom's spirit inside a living person because she was—" I stop.

I think I've caught a bird.

"Yeah," Noah says slowly, finishing my sentence for me because he knows I can't. "You saw your mom while she was trying to get to heaven."

Chapter 17

Missing Out

I think back to the night my mom died. A spirit was inside me. It racked me with chills. It made a desperate attempt to communicate with me, to get me to stop my mom, to save her. And if I had, the spirit inside me would've crossed over. Through me. After we die, we don't get a second chance to right our wrongs, we get a second chance to right *living* people's wrongs, to influence the *living* and get them to do the next right thing. That's how the dead atone. That's how they move on. If only we'll listen.

And the evil ones? If they get us to do the wrong thing, if they toy with us and get us off track, maybe they cross over to—purgatory? Hell? Or do they just linger, tormenting the living for an eternity? I shake my head, trying to shed the thought. Maybe it's not so black and white. Maybe evil spirits have given up on getting people to do the right thing. Maybe that's it. Maybe it's too hard for some. The evil ones aren't really evil; they've just . . . quit.

I think about seeing Mom in the grocery store. Was she trying to get that living woman to buy a gift—bubble bath—for someone? To make amends? To reach out to someone she hadn't spoken to in years? To take better care of her child? Who knows?

Right then, I feel like I pluck another slippery humming-bird from the angry flock. I don't know exactly what Mom was up to in the store, but I suddenly know something else. *She didn't cross over that day.* Whatever my mother was trying to get that woman to do; I don't think it worked. Because I interrupted her. She must have gone back to . . .

"But where *are* they?" I ask Noah. "When they try to cross over through living people and fail? While they're waiting to try again and inhabit another person? In their graves?"

"No," Noah says. "I know that much. That's why the prof lives here. But I don't know how we find them."

WE WALK BACK TOWARD the parking lot where Noah left his car. No one talks. Birds chirp and flit around the gravestones; leaves shuffle in the soft breeze. We make our way over the hill, around the main chapel and head for Noah's Honda.

But that's when we see something . . . or someone. By the car, kind of lingering at the driver's side door. At first, I think someone is trying to break into it. But who does that? Who breaks into a car that's parked at a cemetery while its owner is likely out grieving at a gravesite? It's wrong on so many levels. But then I wonder if maybe it's a priest or something. Maybe a few of them patrol the cemetery, looking for people to comfort. Kate, Noah, and I immediately stop, but Jay takes a few steps farther.

"My god," he whispers. We tiptoe up next to him.

"Is it a priest?" I ask, gripping Jay's arm.

"No," he says. "It's my dad."

And then Jay starts going toward him—fast. We follow. My throat catches when I see that he's right. There, leaning against the Honda, is Jay's alcoholic, famous professor father, holding a rosary in one hand and pouring some sort of oil on the roof rack with the other.

"Dad?" Jay asks. "Is that you?" But when he asks it, he sounds so angry. Angrier than I've ever heard him. The man turns and looks at him, at us. And it's not Jay's dad; it's the madman from the cemetery house with the bushy beard.

"I feel terrible," the man says, moving around the car. "But maybe this will help. This is holy oil. A priest gave it to me once. Said it would help with . . . what I was seeing."

"What are you talking about? Wait. Dad, I saw you. It's me—it's—"

The man stops with the oil. He's staring directly at Jay now. He approaches and I tense. His pale, bony knees protrude through the holes in his stained jeans. He looks into Jay's eyes. "Are you . . . ? My God. Howard's son? Howard Bell?"

Jay nods.

"You—you look just like him." There's a sad twist of a smile under his beard. He glances at the rest of us. "And I'm sorry. I shouldn't have ignored you all at the front door. I should have let you in. And explained. I just didn't want Noah digging it up. Or figuring anything else out. I just . . . I don't want to know any more than I already do. But anyway, I'm sorry."

And that's when I see it. A heartbeat after he says the words *I'm sorry*—I see a flash, like a passing shadow, a shadow I recognize.

"I'd shake your hand but . . ." The man holds up the glass jar of oil and the rosary. "Hands are a little oily. I'm Peter Broomfield. Worked with your dad." His eyes grow rheumy, like he's suddenly drowning in a flood of unwanted memories. He shakes his head softly and then goes back to work on the car, pouring the oil across the top and in a thin line down the back, over the trunk. Some oozes over Noah's NASA bumper stickers.

"He helped your dad find the cross," Noah says.

Peter mumbles something with his back still to us, his voice trailing off as he keeps coating the car. I can barely hear what he's saying. It's something about the oil helping him sleep. How he can't imagine "seeing them" at our age, how it's hard enough at his.

"That should do it," he says, surveying the greasy sheen that now coats Noah's Honda. He glances back toward his house.

"Wait," Jay says. "Don't go—"

"Like I said before," he interrupts. The oil starts dripping down Noah's windshield. "Sorry I was so rude." His gravelly voice sounds as if it might break. He looks at Jay again. "Really sorry . . ."

And with that, a glimpse of Jay's father flashes bright within Peter. As always, I am petrified by the sight of it; I can't imagine ever getting used to it. Peter Broomfield is living proof of that. But I know we all see it now. Maybe even Noah, too, if he tried on the necklace . . .

"Stop talking about this," Jay says, almost frantic. "I don't care about that. What I care about is how I found you in a puddle of blood. When I was *ten*, Dad. Ten. Why'd you have to drink like that? *Why?*"

For a moment, it's just Jay and his dad, standing side-by-side. His dad is so clear, so present, I almost forget what I'm seeing. I tell myself it's his spirit. *Just his spirit.* Then I see only Peter again.

And it hits me. Peter isn't talking about being rude. He's not talking about ignoring us at the door earlier or throwing Noah out of his house.

Peter extends his hand, waiting for a handshake. "I'm sorry," he says again, this time with more determination.

I know what this is. Jay's dad is trying to cross. He's inside Peter, trying to get him to do the right thing, to apologize for losing his temper, for throwing Noah out, for not answering the door, for not helping us. To ask forgiveness. And at the same time, Jay's dad is using Peter to apologize to his son. Jay's father is asking for forgiveness, too, and for so much more.

He waits for a response. Jay stares back, and I see a flash of someone in Jay's place, a glimpse of someone I don't recognize.

"Jay," I say. "A spirit is with you. Listen—"

"Never," Jay snaps, cutting me off. "I'll never forgive what you did." His voice is icy and flat. His dad's head falls, and then he's gone. Peter is all that's left. His eyes are mistier than before, as if he's about to cry. He turns and walks away toward his little cemetery house, rounding the main building. Jay stares after him, as if he looks hard enough he'll see his father walking back this way.

KATE IS THE FIRST one brave enough to speak. I can tell she doesn't have a clue what to say. So she speaks in questions. "I think there's paper towels in Noah's trunk? I'll start wiping off the oil that got on the windshield? Think I'll be cursed if I throw holy-oil-covered paper towels in a trash can?"

None of us answer her and she heads for the car. I don't like what I see in Jay's eyes, or rather what I *don't* see. It's like he's a bird that's flown away and all I'm looking at is the empty nest left behind.

"Jay?" I ask, slowly approaching. "You all right?"

He doesn't respond.

"We'll get you home, okay?" Noah tries next. "Let's get in the car. Let's just go. Get some food. Clear our—"

"Dad was with him," Jay says. His forehead is tightly creased. He's talking something through, not to us, but to himself. "It's like I forgot. I forgot how all this works. I thought I was just talking to my dad, you know? Just for a second, I thought he was . . ."

The words hurt. Physically. They're sharp, like a thousand bee stings to the heart. I wince because I know exactly how Jay feels. When I saw my mom in the grocery store, I was given a gift: I got to believe, just for a second, that she was *here*. That she was *alive*. That all of it—the car wreck, the funeral, the days spent wishing for just one more chance—was an extended bad dream. To think that someone is alive again for even a moment . . . it's amazing, it's all you've wanted. The problem is, once it's over, the pain is just as strong as that joy. Maybe even stronger. It teaches you the true meaning of the saying, "Hurts like hell."

"Peter Broomfield," Noah says softly. "I saw his name mentioned in all your dad's articles. So I contacted him. Way back. I asked him for help figuring this out. Even though they found the cross and the book, they could never figure out that last part. What we did. And he said he didn't want to know. That what he already knows has ruined him enough."

Jay doesn't say anything.

"He's been seeing spirits," Noah continues. "For years. The whole team wore the necklace when they found it. He said it drove most people crazy. Two killed themselves over it. And it's why he lives alone and in a cemetery. Because the spirits aren't with the dead; they're out with the living. He gets the most peace here. He told me everything the team knew. But they didn't figure out what we did. They tried. They stuffed the manuscript back in the cave, hoping it would stop what they were seeing. They didn't even report finding it."

Jay doesn't look at Noah. I'm not sure he's heard a word he's said. "But how did my dad know to be here . . . just now?" he whispers.

Noah takes a few steps closer to Jay. "Ignatius says spirits are drawn to your deepest desires. Your dad must have seen his chance. Peter feels terrible and so did your dad, Jay."

"Your dad saw his chance," I add. "To apologize to *you*."

Jay shakes his head. "This can't be right. Can't be. Does this mean my dad was right about everything? He was a drunk. And . . . I mean, are the *Catholics* right about everything? I mean if they know how people cross and all . . ."

"No," Noah says firmly. "That's the one thing I learned from Peter. He told me that there are signs of this hidden everywhere, in every tradition, all over. He said there are quotes from the Buddha about discerning evil spirits. And there's a line in the *Bhagavad Gita* about spirits and knowing what to do and what not to do. It's not a Christian thing; it's a *human* thing. Ignatius was a *mystic*. And that's what mystics are always on about. It's big picture, universal shit."

Jay's face darkens. "Yeah, well, it doesn't really matter how true it is. My dad's a coward," he says, kicking some of the gravel. "Couldn't make anything right in life. Had to wait til death." He steps toward Noah's Honda and climbs in the backseat and slams the door—hard.

"This is not good," Noah says.

"Yeah," Kate says, chewing her nails. "I've got nothing but

wads of holy-oily paper towels. How do we make this better? The only tool I have is gum. All these crises have been draining my supply. I'm down to two flavors."

"Let's just go," I say to Noah. "Just . . . keep talking to him. Okay? We only have about a thirty-minute car ride home. Kate and I will follow in the Camaro."

"Wait," Noah says. "You'll follow in the *what?*"

I scrunch my face in my best non-verbal *I'm sorry* and point down the hill. The Camaro sits under the tree where I left it, perched on the side of the road near a group of gravestones like evidence of a joyride gone very, very wrong.

"I'm sorry," I say. "We had to follow you. And the Wagon would've given us away."

"If my best friend weren't freaking out right now, I might stop to flip out about this. But, you had your reasons. Besides . . ." Noah points at Jay in the Honda; Jay has his head in his hands in the back seat. "We need to go. Just please, with every fiber of my being, I beg of you: do not wreck my dad's car."

I FIRE UP THE Camaro and wait for Noah to drive past us. Then I make a U-turn in the narrow cemetery road and follow him. Kate doesn't reach for the radio; we just watch the road in the silence. We drive and drive. Part of me wishes we could just drive forever.

But just before we reach I-77, Noah pulls over. We follow and pull up behind him. Jay jumps out and jogs back to the Camaro. I roll down the window, and he leans in close, puts his hands on my door. I swallow. I can see the whites of his eyes around his pupils. He looks disturbed. Mad, like Peter Broomfield at the cemetery. Like he was lost, and now that he's found, he's crazed.

"You saw a spirit inside me too, didn't you? Back there?" He's talking way too fast, but I nod. "That's what I thought. Because I got chills. And this sinking feeling. And I knew what I was supposed to do." He pushes away from the car, kicks at the dirt on the side of the road. I get out and reach for him but hesitate at the last second.

"I was supposed to say something like *it's okay, Pops. I forgive you. Blah-blah-blah.* Like the end of a Pixar movie. But I couldn't, Riley. I just couldn't. Okay?" He says it like he's mad . . . like he's mad at *me.*

I rack my brain for a response as the cars whiz by us on the road, cold reminders that no matter what happens, no matter who or what you lose, time and people and life just keep going. I search for something positive, something to make him feel better about seeing his dad, about what his dad said. "He must have been really sorry, Jay. Your dad got Peter to feel it, and your dad felt it, too. Peter's eyes were all red and watery and—"

"Stop," Jay says. He leans over and puts his hands on his thighs. Like he might throw up. But he doesn't. He just stands there, bent over with his head half-hanging into the street. We're engulfed in a horrible silence that's broken only by the swooshing sounds of cars.

"You all right?" Noah asks, jogging up. Kate joins now, too. Noah puts a hand on Jay's back. "Jay?"

Jay straightens up and looks at Noah and then at Kate and then at me. "Peter did the right thing," he says slowly. "My dad got him to do the right thing. He apologized. He did it. Which means Peter was my dad's doorway. My dad *crossed.* So now he's . . ."

The silence swallows us again. We wait and wait for what feels like hours. I want to run out into the street, stop the traffic. *Stop.* I want to tell them all. *Just stop.* But I don't. And I also don't say what I'm thinking, what must be dawning on Jay, too.

Your dad is gone. Forever. And you missed your last chance.

"You guys," Jay says, panic filling his eyes. "What have I done?"

Chapter 18

Silly Buoys

The look on Jay's face as he realizes his dad is gone is terrifying. But so is the idea that his dad is *really gone.* Forever this time.

Jay gets in the Camaro for the ride back. He refuses to talk the whole way home. We exit at Brecksville, turn down the main drag. Kate does her best to cheer him up. It doesn't help. She suggests going to her basement to debrief. He refuses. She suggests that we all go to his house for video games, but he refuses that, too. Then he starts saying he's okay, and I keep telling him that he's not. And that he shouldn't be alone right now.

He tells me to drive him to his house. Angrily. I know that if I don't, he'll just walk the whole way himself.

"Jay, please, think of this," Kate says, trying a last-ditch effort to comfort him. "He got Peter to do what he was supposed to. He got his old friend to apologize to us. And your dad apologized to you, too. And he crossed. Which means he's definitely a good spirit, not a bad one."

"It's okay. You don't have to say all this," he says. His voice is a monotone.

I pull up in front of his house, and he gets out. Kate and I do, too. Noah pulls up behind us in the Honda and joins us. Kate and Noah give him hugs, and even Noah's is a real one—not one of those guy hugs where they sort of bump chests and pound each other's backs once or twice. He clings to Jay. Now it's my turn. And I hold him tight.

But he's not hugging back. It feels like I'm holding a statue, cold and unyielding. Finally, I let go, and he slowly walks toward his front door.

"Bye?" I say to his back. He turns and looks at all of us.

"I'm no good at this, am I?"

"Good at what?" I ask, even though I don't need to.

"At listening. At paying attention, to the spirits."

"I think it just takes practice," I say. "Time. I . . ."

But Jay's not listening. He turns around, takes the front porch stairs two at a time and disappears inside. The front door closes behind him. I want to open it again; I want to follow him, hold him longer. Except that now I'm thinking about what he said, about being bad at listening to spirits. I think about the spirit I saw in him when all this started, when he was texting Sarah after we'd visited my mom's gravesite. I think about Jay poring over his dad's archeology articles, crawling into a dark, dank cave, looking for something his dad spent his whole life trying to find. And yet, when Jay got the chance with his dad, he let it slip by.

And suddenly, I feel tired. So. Tired.

Tired of waiting for him. Tired of hoping he'll read the signs and see that I should be more than a friend. And maybe I shouldn't be. We're both damaged, easy targets for evil spirits to mess with. And maybe that's it. Maybe that's why I've liked him for so long; maybe it's no more complicated or romantic than that the damaged are drawn to the damaged. Connected by hurt. And something hits me then, too: a truth that maybe I've always known but has lingered just at the edge of my consciousness, like one of those imaginary hummingbirds I couldn't quite catch back at the cemetery.

I'm tired of liking someone who is just as bad at listening for spirits as I am.

AFTER I DROP NOAH and Kate off, I drive home. I tiptoe into the house and find my father dozing on the couch. I gently touch his shoulder.

"Riley," he says with a start. "What time is it? I hope my pot roast hasn't dried out. Wait." He rubs his eyes. "*Where* have you been?"

"I'm sorry," I say. I curl up on the other end of the couch by his feet.

He looks shocked that I'm sitting with him. The last time he saw me I was all freaked out about walking in on his date with Sammy, and now I'm crawling onto the sofa like we're best friends. I think he wants to yell at me for skipping school, but my couch move has caught him off guard, rendered him defenseless. I almost know what's coming next.

"You want soup?" he asks. "I made tomato artichoke."

I smile and shake my head no.

He waits another minute. "You're not pregnant are you?"

I smile, bigger this time. "No, Pops. Not even close."

"Oh, thank god." He looks at me. Asking. "But . . . you're okay?"

I nod, hoping he buys it. And even though it's a warm night, I reach for the red blanket on the back of the couch and pull it around my shoulders. I'm cold.

And covered in chills.

The pit in my stomach is unmistakable. I picture the spirit I saw with the kids at air band practice, the one in the red flapper dress. I imagine her with me now, twirling around in my ribcage, her sequins slamming into my heart and lungs. I think about what Noah said today about spirits, how they are most active around your deepest desires.

Stop, I tell myself. *Remember that you've been given a gift. So stop and listen. What do you hear?*

And I guess I sort of know. The answer isn't all that hard. It's just . . . I should say something to Dad, to tell him what I know. But how? Maybe I should just tell him what I want. And what I want is to believe that even if he gets a girlfriend or gets married again, that we'll be just as close, that he'll still worry about me all the time, that he'll still peer into my eyes and make sure I'm okay from the inside out. That he'll still run around offering me eggs and soups and muffins at all hours of the day or night. But maybe he won't. Maybe the strongest connection to my dad and even to Jay and Kate and Noah is through grief, and if any of us get over the hurt—really get over it—what keeps us all tied together will be snipped like a ribbon on a birthday present.

Then say all that, I urge myself. *Say it.*

"I guess, it's just that . . ." I pause and sit up, letting the blanket slide off my shoulders. I eye the front door because I know I'm going to feel like running as soon as I'm done. But I take a deep breath. "I'm . . . freaked out."

Dad's watching me like I'm a patient in the ICU about to get yanked off life support. He actually looks *frightened.* It's awful.

"Um," he says slowly, his eyes a little wide, totally unsure of what to do with New Confessional Daughter. "If you wouldn't mind explaining. What is it that you're freaked out about?"

Say it. Now it's too late. *SAY IT.* The twinge in my gut is back again. Every time I think of stopping, it's like buckets of water are smashing against a stone wall. I have to keep going. I have to.

"It's just that," I pause and look down at the blanket, so afraid that I've figured this all out. "I'm afraid that what makes me matter is all the bad stuff."

He blinks several times. "I don't understand. What bad stuff, Riley?"

"I mean, you and me, are we close because of who we lost? And Jay, are we tight for the same reason? Because we both lost parents? Is that all there is?" I look up at my dad. My eyes finally blur with the tears that have been two years in the making, but I keep going. "And if we get over it. What then? If you move on from Mom, will you move on from me, too? And then will I be . . . *alone?*"

As soon as I say the word *alone*—right now, in this moment, I know something new—that my deepest fear isn't that we'll never get over losing Mom, my biggest fear is that we *will*. And Dad will move on and bail out and shack up with some other family. And I'll be some sort of quasi-orphan. And maybe *I'll* even get over losing her, and then I won't really feel connected to Dad, and just as bad, I won't feel connected to Jay, or to Noah, or to Kate, either. My friends, my *family*—that's what they are, too, in just as real a way as Dad—won't get me anymore, and I won't get them, and the glue that binds us all together will be gone . . . and then what?

"Oh, Riley."

That's all he says. I can tell he's drumming up the courage to talk about it all, and I brace myself for a food analogy. I expect him to say something like dating as a widower is like

burning a new casserole you've never cooked before. Or that
life without Mom is like cooking with an electric stove when
you're used to a gas one. I prepare to receive offers of parsnips and al dente pasta. Hear another plug for the fresh corn
bread and pot roast he has in the kitchen.

"Do you know what a channel buoy is? For boats?" he asks.

I shake my head no. Mostly I'm shocked. A boating metaphor? I guess I'm not the only Strout who's capable of
surprises.

"Well," Dad says. "A channel buoy is a big metal stand
with a light on it, or with a bright orange or green sign. It
floats in the water, in the ocean or in a big lake." He looks
straight at me as he speaks. I'm not sure I've ever seen him
look so serious. "It's anchored, so it never drifts. A buoy tells
the boaters where the channel is, where they should steer so
they can come into port. Safe. Out of the wind. It's tied to
the bottom *real* tight. Storms come through, boats bump into
them, but the buoy doesn't move; it's always there, always
telling people how to get home. That's a channel buoy. Ever
seen one?"

"Yeah," I say, staring back at him. "I think so."

He nods, reaching across the blanket to take my hands.
"Well, the way I feel about you is just like that. Everything else
in my life can change: my job, my kitchen, my silly hobbies."
He pauses. "Even a girlfriend. But not how I feel about you,
Riley. That doesn't change. It can't. Not ever. Just like that
buoy. It's tied down *tight.*"

For the first time in a very long time (maybe ever), I actually stop to think about something my Dad just said. *Tied
down tight. Doesn't drift. Safe.*

"You know what? You really have a way with analogies."
And the look on his face when I say that—it's a thousand

times more awesome than when I tell him I love his Special
Plate Breakfasts. "And I love you, too."

Now I have a feeling that's totally different than when
spirits have come before. It's not like when my friends fed
me beef jerky and cigarettes and got it all wrong. It feels different than when I was in the elevator with Jay, when I was just
trying everything that popped into my head. No, something
has changed; something has left me. Something has flown.
But instead of emptiness or absence, I feel a crash of relief.

Or maybe not flown, exactly. No, if Dad can move beyond
food to buoys, I can put the hummingbirds to rest, too.

Because I think I'm a doorway. That just opened up.

I MANAGE TO SLEEP pretty well. I don't know whether it was
the cemetery trip, or what we saw Jay go through, or plain old
exhaustion, but whatever it was—I sleep okay. When I wake
up, I text Jay to see how he's doing. I wait for his usual immediate text back. But nothing comes. Then I call. No answer. I
text again. Nothing.

Oh, God, no, I think. I really can't handle another disap-
pearance right now. Haven't we all learned that none of us
can go AWOL again?

I try Noah and Kate. Neither one has heard from him. I
tell them I'll come pick them up so we can go over and check
on him on our way to school. He's probably still asleep, that
he's probably just exhausted, wiped out, that the phone
isn't waking him. This is what I tell myself. But worry starts
gnawing at me, slow and steady.

After a shower, I pull on some jeans and a tee and walk over
to the sink to brush my teeth. On the way, I step on something. It hurts like crazy, like I've stepped on a thumbtack. I

pick up my foot and see an earring. It's a big silver knot. And it isn't mine. And it isn't Kate's.

Sammy.

I lean over the sink, afraid for an instant that I'm going to vomit. I try to calm down and stare at my blurry reflection in the steamy bathroom mirror. My mind races in a thousand different directions. But mostly, I'm thinking about what my dad said about the channel buoy. I want to believe him, I really do . . . and I know I should. I look at myself again in the mirror, at my heaving chest, my terrified eyes. And I feel something. Something *familiar.* Something *known.*

"You're okay, Riley," I say in a whisper to myself. I look deeply into my hazel eyes and at the fear that blankets my face like the steam on the mirror. "You're okay," I say again. Chills make their way up my arms and legs. And then an idea comes to me. It feels good, it feels nuts; it feels . . . *right.*

I'm still staring at myself in the mirror, my breath coming in quick bursts, when I hear my cell. It's a text. Kate and Noah are on the front porch. They got antsy and drove over. I get myself together and the feeling passes. I head down the stairs and open the door to see Kate and Noah standing there, waiting for me. Noah's wearing a T-shirt printed with the words *I Miss Pluto.* His eyes meet mine and communicate everything.

"I know," I say with a sad smile. "I'm worried about him, too."

Chapter 19

Family Rule Extension

The moment we climb into the car, it fills with the sounds of worrying. Noah clicks the door lock in the backseat, I tap the steering wheel as I drive, and Kate digs in her purse beside me. She finds a pack of Flaming Grape gum and hands out pieces to each of us. For once, Noah and I chomp as loudly as she does.

"I saw, like, three different spirits in my dad last night," Kate announces through her gum wad. "I think they were all trying to get him to apologize to my mom for being the worst husband in all of recorded history. Of course he didn't."

I catch Noah's eyes in the rearview mirror. "Did you end up wearing the necklace? You know, when you had it?"

He leans up and rests his chin on the back of my seat. "No. I was tempted, but Peter warned me off it. Said it would drive me crazy, like him. That maybe it would be easier to hear Cam if I wasn't freaking out, you know?"

Kate digs in her purse and gets out more gum. She shoves two more pieces in her mouth. "Is that what's going to happen to *us*?" she asks. "I really, really don't want to end up as the old lady version of *that* guy. Would we all end up living together in a cemetery? Although we could probably parlay that into a reality TV series. We'd be rich. Rich and *cray-cray.*"

"I wouldn't worry," Noah says with a gentle laugh. "We won't let it. I mean, think about it: a team of professors couldn't decipher the Magis section in the manuscript. But we did. We can figure out how to make this stop if we keep looking. It's like the word says. There's always more, you know?"

The old lump in my throat appears out of nowhere. Noah leans back. Something burns inside me right then, and I stop my whirling thoughts and listen. What I feel is the urge to climb over the seats and hug Noah more tightly than I've ever hugged anyone. For always lightening the mood, for pulling us back from a total freak-out, for being so full of hope. The feeling I have is . . . just what he said. It's *more.* I want to ask Kate and Noah to look at me; I want to know if a spirit is here. But I think I already know.

"I hope you're right, Noah," Kate says softly. . . "I hope you're right."

JAY'S SHADE IS PULLED down. And he never has it pulled down.

"End times," Kate pronounces. She blows and pops a bubble. "This is *bad.*"

She knocks on the glass. No answer. She tries again. Nothing.

"Front door?" Noah suggests.

"I haven't gone through the front door in, like, *forever*," I say. "But let's try."

We hurry around to the front and Noah rings the bell. No answer. Two more rings. Nothing. He tries the door, and it's locked. Dread fills every part of me. Something's wrong. Maybe he just wants to be alone? Or maybe he's decided to bail and run away? Or worse, has he—

"Wait," I say, looking at Noah. "Didn't Jay say you know where they hide a key?"

He's already headed straight for the garden, and overturns a little concrete mushroom sculpture. "Bingo," he says, pulling a key from under the stem.

I really am genuinely shocked that Jay told only Noah about the key. Though I suppose I shouldn't be. I guess we all have secrets, every one of us.

Noah puts the key in the lock and turns. We carefully step inside.

"Jay?" Noah calls. "Mrs. Bell? Hello?"

No answer. We step into the kitchen, then the living room. We head to Jay's bedroom and the door is closed. My stomach clenches. *He was so upset about his dad. We should've gone home with him; we shouldn't have let him be alone.* Noah pushes the door open slowly, and I hold my breath. But he's not here. His laptop is open on his bed; some books are strewn around the floor. His bed is made and there's no wallet on the dresser.

"Call his phone again," I say. "See if it rings, if he's left it in here somewhere."

Kate dials but we don't hear anything. He must have his phone with him. Then why isn't he answering it?

"Where the *hell* is he?" Kate asks. "And why do our guy friends insist on disappearing all the time? Is this a boy thing I don't know about? Disappearing?"

"Anybody know his password?" Noah asks as he sits on the bed. He's turned on Jay's laptop, but it's locked. I crawl on the bed next to him and wager a guess.

"Pink Floyd?" I say.

"Nope," Noah says after typing it into the password box.

"Totally-clueless-sometimes?" Kate jokes, with no humor in her voice.

Noah moves over just an inch, his hip touching mine. "Here," he says, moving his shoulder even closer. "I'll be your pillow. Rest while I try about a billion passwords. You look tired."

So I do. I rest my head on his shoulder and immediately feel guilty because I get the tiniest urge to just . . . stay there.

"Should we really be trying to get into his computer?" I ask. "I feel bad."

"We're worried about him," Kate says. "This is just the technology extension of the Family Rule. If we're seriously worried about you, we get to hack into your accounts."

After blessing Noah's hacking efforts, she starts snooping through Jay's drawers and shelves. Noah tries and fails at password after password. Finally, I force myself off the bed and pace. I accidentally run my toe into Jay's guitar and knock it over. And I hear the clinking of glass. Three mostly empty beer bottles roll across the floor.

"You guys," I say, holding them up and sniffing inside. They smell fresh. There's still a little beer in the bottom of each one. "I think Jay's been drinking."

"Drinking?" Noah says, looking up from the computer. "He decides it's a good idea to *drink*? At eight in the morning?"

"Yeah," Kate says, "that's like super cliché. Like a repeating-family-patterns lecture in health class."

I don't know what to say. She's right. He's always said his dad's drinking is what ruined his whole life. So now he wants to do it, too? I lean down and pick up the guitar. As I put it upright again, memories of Jay playing Pink Floyd on a loop flood my mind. And I have an idea.

"Try this," I say. "*Wishuwerehere.* No spaces."

Noah types away.

"Bingo," he says. He flashes a goofy grin at me, but it fades just as fast. The screen lights up. "Let's see. Browser history. This morning Jay searched his dad's name, a few of his dad's archeology books, and Dick's Sporting Goods."

"He's upset and missing his dad, so he's drinking," Kate said. "But what could he possibly want at Dick's? Unless they sell guitar strings now?"

"Let's start there," I say. "Something isn't right."

Noah sighs and closes the laptop. "So. Looks like we're skipping school again, huh?"

DICK'S SPORTING GOODS IS a remarkable place in that it makes you feel like a slacker the second you walk in. It's massive and freezing and smells like a giant, brand new sneaker. It practically commands you to get in shape. There's aisle after aisle of outdoorsy stuff—tents, lanterns, fishing gear, rolling coolers, survival kits—arranged as if to induce maximum guilt and to tell you that the people who matter are *outside* all the time, doing all these amazing granola-bar-commercial things. If these tents could talk, I know what they'd say: *Why aren't you tromping up a mountain and breathing the thin air of high-altitude victory, like all the awesome people?*

In my defense, I do have an activity. And it drains me physically and emotionally. But I don't need a four-hundred-dollar backpack to listen for spirits inside my body and try to figure out what they want from me. I wonder what equipment Dick's could sell for this St. Ignatius spirit-listening sport. Earplugs and blinders so you can listen to the departed even in the worst of conditions? Spirit mood rings that change color depending on who's inhabiting you? Psych ward survival kits for when spirit discernment finally gets the best of you?

"Jay!" Noah calls out as we search the store. No one answers. We do get a few annoyed looks from the employees, however. I can't blame them. It's obvious we're not here to stock up for a camping trip.

"Guys?" Kate says. "This is the portable camp toilet aisle. I don't think he'd be *here.*"

I head for the exit. "Yeah, let's go." Maybe he decided to run away, or camp out under the stars? Maybe he came here for a sleeping bag and a lantern? But my worst fear is that he feels so awful about not forgiving his father that he's looking for something more permanent than gear for some time away. Like a rope to fashion a noose. I shake the thought from my head.

"OMG they sell bags you can poop in," Kate says as she meets me by the door. "Is it wrong that part of me wants to try one?"

"Yes. Wrong," Noah says, joining us. "Very, very wrong."

"Jay!" I call out again, desperate.

Noah places his hand on my arm. "He's not here, Riley. Let's try school."

AFTER SCOURING THE SCHOOL parking lot for his car, we drive off before we get spotted and cruise all over town looking. We try his favorite spots: Vintage Vinyl, Patchman's Music Shop. We drive along the river, looking for his car ditched by the road; we drive slowly down the main drag of Brecksville. When we don't find him at the bagel place or any of the fast food joints, we exchange silent glances.

This is bad, I say to myself again.

I think back to what Kate said earlier, about how the boys in our family disappear. She's right; Kate and I have been the most stable ones throughout this whole ordeal. Which makes me sort of proud. And question the stereotype about girls freaking out in a crisis. As far as I can tell, the typical guy response to an emergency is to bail. My Dad, up until last night, anyway, fit that category, too.

"What now?" Kate asks from the passenger seat.

"I don't know," I say. "I don't know where else to look."

We pull off the main drag and I absently head back home. But a funny thing happens. When I pass the sign for Arthur's Autobody—the white paint perennially filthy and peeling, its logo featuring two guys in overalls tugging at either side of a broken engine—I can't help but think of the boys: Noah on one side and Jay on another.

And I remember coming once here with Mom, too, when our car needed a repair. Wandering down the aisles, staring up at all the silly dashboard decorations . . .

And all at once I am reminded of what I felt last night. I am a door that has just opened.

Now, maybe, I think I have a glimpse of what's on the other side. "I think I need to run into Arthur's," I hear myself say.

"In *where?*" Kate asks.

"Arthur's," I say pointing at the sign. Even though we're all worried about Jay, I have to follow through with this. And I have to do it now. "You coming?"

"Um, why?" Noah asks from the backseat. "My dad got a set of radial tires from them and was totally ripped off."

I hop out and dash into the store without answering. There are racks of air fresheners, bumper stickers, and little things to hang from your rearview mirror. I see miniature dice, beads, and even rosaries. But I know exactly what I'm looking for; I saw it all those years ago with Mom. I approach the counter and speak to the bald dude behind it. His shirt is embroidered with the name Stan.

"Excuse me," I say. "Um, Stan? I'm looking for—"

"Car broke down?" he interrupts. "Cause mechanics have all gone home for the day."

"It's not even lunchtime yet," Noah moans as he joins me at the counter. "And do you know a Mr. Digman? Because he's my dad. And he bought a set of radials in here about a—"

"*Noah*," I whisper, elbowing him in the side.

"My car didn't break down," I explain to Stan. "I'm looking for something for my dashboard. You know those little-bobble things? A hula girl. I saw one in here once."

"A what?" Stan asks.

"You know, those little hula girls that jiggle when you drive? You stick them on the dash? You used to have them . . ."

"Oh, yeah," Stan says gruffly. "I think we still have one. But she's broke. Took her off the shelves a while ago. She's in the back. Hang on." He disappears through a Staff Only door that swings in his wake.

"Why are we getting a hula girl?" Kate whispers.

"I'll explain later."

Stan reappears with a small ratty box. He opens it up and pulls out the even rattier looking hula girl. Still, she's pretty much as I remember her: she has long frazzled black hair, a chipped red bikini top, and a frayed hula skirt. And she's in one piece.

"Sell her to you for three bucks," Stan says.

"Wait," Kate says. She takes the hula girl and turns her over. "Riley, do we need her to stick on the dash? Like, do we need this hula girl to be functional? Because the sticky stuff on the bottom is totally not sticky anymore."

"Excellent eye," I say. I turn back to Stan. "Throw in some duct tape and you've got a deal."

"Deal," Stan says. He roots around under the counter and pulls out a big roll of silver duct tape. He pulls off a couple of inches, loops it back on itself and slaps it on the bottom of the hula girl. "There," he says. "She'll stick like glue and jiggle like a crazy woman."

"She's perfect." I hand over the money.

WE RIDE BACK TO my house in silence. We've run out of places to look for Jay, and we've run out of ideas. I know what we're all afraid of.

After I cut the engine, we sit in the car. "You don't think?" Noah says. "I mean, he was so upset when we left. But he wouldn't do anything crazy . . . would he?"

Kate sighs. "*Why* couldn't he just forgive his dad? Or at least hug him or something." She opens her door. But she doesn't get out. "So, what do we do now?"

"If you guys don't hear from him in another hour . . . call the cops," I say.

"What do you mean 'you guys'? You going somewhere?" Noah asks from the back.

"Yes," I say. "And can you hand me the hula girl?"

Noah hands the doll to me, and I slap her on the dash. I gently flick her hips. As promised, she shakes like crazy.

"She works," I say with a half-smile.

Noah eyes me in the rearview. Suspicious. "You all right?" he asks.

I reach up and softly bat at Mom's hummingbird necklace that's hanging from the rearview mirror. The sunshine glints off the silver bird charm. "I am now," I say. "Be back soon. And text me ASAP if you hear from Jay."

"We'll keep looking," Kate says. She starts to get out but then stops and glares at me. "Riley?" she says softly.

"Yeah?"

"So, taking off right now?" she says. "It kind of sucks. With Jay gone and everything else."

I nod, summoning my resolve. And look back at the hummingbird necklace. Watch it sway in the sunlight. "You're right," I say. "But I promise I'm not disappearing. This doesn't count as a bail; I'll be right back."

"Okay," Kate says slowly. She pulls in a deep breath. "But before you go, I just want to say sorry."

The charm swings back and forth. Back and forth. Like it's keeping time to music I can't hear. "But why? You're not the one who's taking off right now."

"Not this time," she says. "But earlier. After you'd just seen your mom. And I'd seen Aunt Lilly. And all I could think about was being invited to join *air band*. I was a cool-girl suck-up. Which is totally a form of bailing on you. Just like Jay did."

I look away from the necklace, and that's when I see it. A flitting spirit behind her eyes.

"So," she says slowly. "Like I said, I'm . . . sorry." Then she gives me this shaky little smile. She wipes her eyes so I can't see that she's teary, but I do. And then the shadow and the flickers are gone. I'm looking at Kate again. At my best girl-friend. Clear as day.

I hadn't thought about it all that much, about her attempt to join air band. But she's right. It was a crappy thing that both Kate and Jay did. It sucked to sit there and watch them take off toward the safety of cool-girl shores, while I was beached with Noah in the audience. At least Noah stayed behind; at least he didn't bail on me and my totally broken self.

I catch sight of his blue eyes in the rearview mirror. He's watching me.

I look back at Kate. And I know something about her. About our friendship. I know that after living through the torture of Back on Track classes and counseling, after accepting so many days of lunch detention in solidarity like the screwups we are, after surviving Mother's Days with mounds and mounds of gum—I know, deep down in my messed-up heart that she'd have to do a lot more to wreck our friendship than try to join air band.

"Forgiven," I say. "Totally and completely." I wonder if she felt what I just saw. "And did you . . . feel something just now?"

Her eyes get wide. A little fearful. "Why? Did you scc—?"

I nod. "Yeah."

Noah leans into the front seat. "What did it feel like?"

"Um," Kate says, looking at the hula girl, her grass skirt still as stone. "I guess I was just thinking about that day, about what we'd seen, and how much all of us have been through. Like, everything—the deaths, the funerals, the tanking grades, all of it—and now this. You know? And I got this *pit* in my stomach."

"Like water hitting a stone?" Noah asks softly, his voice full of wonder.

Kate tilts her head and gives him a puzzled smile through her tears. "Yeah. Exactly like that. And I knew I needed to apologize for taking off that day. For the whole air band thing. I just . . . knew it. Does that make any sense?"

Of course it does. A spirit just moved her, gave her a little jolt, a sign pointing the way. And she got it. She did what it wanted her to do. She squeezes my arm as she gets out of the car. Noah follows but lingers by the driver's side door and my open window.

"If you need us," he says, "just text. We'll be there in a heartbeat."

I DRIVE DOWN FITZWATER Road, past Jay's house, and then head toward the Cuyahoga River. I stop just before the bridge, ease the car over to the side of the road and put it in park. I look again at the hummingbird necklace hanging from the rearview mirror. It's been the reminder I've felt I've needed all this time: *You aren't allowed to be happy. Not after all the heartache you caused.*

That's when I feel it: chills all over my body. A sinking feeling so strong, it seems like falling. Goose bumps run so fast along my skin they almost sting. I sit like that, letting my feelings and thoughts bash into each other, letting them do whatever they need to do. I wait, quietly, for the truth to come. And it does. Like Noah says, it feels like a drop of water gently hitting a sponge, an idea that soaks into my bones, that fits just right, that frees me to move on.

I know exactly why I've never been able to take a joyride in my car, blast music, or let the wind whip through the open windows since Mom died. It's that I don't want to live and be happy if being happy means that I've gotten over her, gotten over losing her, moved on like she was just a passing thought. Her loss has become my connection to my dad, to my friends, to the world. It's almost become who I am. Almost.

I'm filled with the urge to take the necklace down. I gently pull it off the mirror and hold it in my hand. I open the car door and walk to the center of the bridge. I lean against the green railing and watch the rushing water far below. Leaves and logs and crests of little waves pass underneath me. And like the river, a thought runs through my mind, fast and strong and unstoppable:

She was so focused on what was missing, that she missed what she had. That was the mistake. Not you, I tell myself. *You . . . were the gift.*

I think about St. Ignatius's secret, about how people leave this life and go on to the next. They don't cross if we don't pay attention. They get stuck if we don't do the things we're destined for. And I think about waiting. Waiting to live my life. Waiting for the pain to stop. Waiting around for Jay to like me. Waiting so long to tell him how I feel. Waiting to move on.

"Missing my life is no way to remember you," I whisper. "Living is."

I pull the bird charm gently to my lips and give it a kiss. I extend my arm and let the necklace dangle above the rushing water below.

And I let it go.

The silver chain arches and bends as it hurtles toward the water. There's a tiny splash when it hits the river and then it disappears beneath the murky water. The same feeling I had earlier when I was at home staring in the mirror floods me again. It's familiar, it's known. I know exactly who's here.

Mom.

Her spirit is with me: fluttery, electric. And I know exactly what she wants me to do next.

I walk back to the car and slide behind the driver's seat. The necklace that has decorated the car for the past two years is now gone, and the only thing left is my hula girl. I give her hips a gentle nudge and she shakes like a crazy woman.

Go.

I turn on the radio. Loud. Then I roll down the windows. The music blares through the car speakers, and I pull the elastic out of my bun and let my hair tumble over my shoulders like kids filling a playground at recess. Unruly. Free. I dig around in the middle of the console and find the sunglasses I never wear and put them on. I check to make sure no one's coming and then hit the gas pedal.

And with my mother inside my very own soul, we take a joyride. The wind whistles through the windows, tangling my hair. The hula girl goes crazy when I hit a bumpy patch. I keep my eyes on the road, but notice how big and bright and blue the sky is. I notice the smell of the summer air, how good it feels as my hair tickles my neck and shoulders. I catch sight of myself in the rearview mirror. I see glimpses of my mother behind my eyes. The best parts of her. The best parts of me. And I see something else I haven't seen in a long, long time.

Happiness looks good on you, Riley.

My heart flutters like hula girl hips, and I feel a brief brushing light of forgiveness, a revelation that nobody should take it all back. A thought that life is complicated, that sometimes our dreams don't turn out like we planned, but that it's worth it. That I was worth it. That life is bigger than loss.

I feel my mother's spirit, like my heart is bursting with joy. And she's not making me feel guilty. She's not scolding me for letting her go that night. For not having all the answers, for not always knowing what to do. She's not making me feel like a mistake. Right now, in this car, I *do* feel like a gift to her, like I was the most-known twist of her very own soul.

After this moment, I will not wonder if I should not have been; I will not wonder if my mother could have only known joy in her life if I hadn't been in it. And if I ever have a daughter of my own, she will not grow up with these doubts. She won't wonder if I'm unhappy because she isn't good enough. Because I will be happy. I will live. I will listen. I will not miss this life.

Mom wants it for me, too. I know it. She wants me to end this feeling of not good enough; she wants me to refuse to pass down some legacy of sadness, to finally stand up and live the life I've been given, whatever it looks like, however it turns out. To trust that there will be signs to point the way. I edge a few miles past the speed limit and . . .

Goodbye, Riley.

And then I feel it, the tear that creeps out of my eye, that slides all the way down my cheek, the one that I know means Mom is gone. It's like a rush of wind slipping through an open door, and that door is me. My tears double and then triple, falling onto my jean shorts and soaking into the denim. I pull the car off the highway and come to a stop on the side of the road. I turn the music down.

I look up through the windshield into the summer Midwestern sky and imagine my mother hovering above me, flying, finally free. On her way, crossing from this life to the next. Through me. I hold my breath, terrified, waiting for the familiar hollowness in my bones, a dark, vacant cave as the wonderful *fullness* I feel in my soul disappears.

The pain does come, but it's followed by something unexpected. There's no guilt. I put my hand to my chest, let the tears fall one after the other—and I smile. In that true way, in that lived-through-it way, I know what I know: That to live and be happy doesn't mean I've forgotten her; it means the exact opposite—that I've remembered.

I drop my head to the steering wheel. I let the tears come; I don't fight a single drop. My mother just left this world, and my new gift has taught me that the best thing to do is to just *feel it.* Not to live like my life depends on it, but to live like someone's afterlife does. To be one of the *portae ad caelum* that's open, always open. I grip the wheel hard and let all of it wash over me, a jumble of feelings like madness in my heart—sadness, anger, emptiness, fullness, peace. Joy.

Goodbye, Mom. Goodbye.

I DON'T KNOW HOW long I sit there like that, just listening to the wind, to the cars, to the first sounds of a world my mother has finally left. Over and over I think how I'm so grateful to have what I have. It won't drive me crazy, the way it did Peter Broomfield, maybe even Jay's father. How could it? I know to listen for spirits, to try to discern all the feelings they give me. To notice the little nudges, the signs on my way. I learned how to speak spirit, how to hear what my mother needed say. And I learned it just in time to be her doorway.

A sound breaks through the soft music on the radio.

A text. I get a text.

I look around for my phone and can't find it. I hear the bing-bong text noise again and realize it has fallen under my seat. I dig around and run my hand over a few stray pens and gum wrappers, but finally pull the phone free. It lights up as I touch the screen.

The message is from Noah.

Found Jay. At The Fields. Get over here fast.

Chapter 20

Bat Boy

The Fields. It's a massive complex of public sports fields: soccer, tennis, softball. But mainly, it's a baseball place. There are seven baseball diamonds total. We hadn't checked it before because I've never known Jay to go there. Plus, it's always locked up tight. Jay would've had to break in. Or jump the fence. It's insanely high. It makes the cemetery fence look like a kiddie gate.

I turn the ignition key and start the car, trying to imagine what Jay is doing at The Fields at least three beers in. Horrible images sail through my mind like arcing baseballs. I imagine him hanging from the stands or unconscious in the dugout. I hit the gas.

"Please, Jay," I whisper as I steer the Wagon back onto the road. "Please be okay."

The drive feels like it takes forever, and I feel so tired—from saying goodbye to Mom, from watching Jay miss his dad, from all this *feeling everything* all the time—but finally, only ten minutes later, I pull into the parking lot and text Noah:

Here.

How do I get in? Climb over?

No answer. So I text one more time.

No answer again.

I hurry to the edge of the parking lot, looking for a way in. The gravel crunches under my shoes. I look down and see wads of gum and random food wrappers of all kinds. I come to the fence around the tennis court and spot a hole cut into the metal. Little bits of fence are clipped and pulled back.

Why here, Jay? Why here?

I bend down and squeeze through. The metal pulls at my T-shirt and I get a few tiny cuts on my arm. I run a hand over the scrapes as I look around and get my bearings. In the distance, I see the baseball diamonds and start walking. I pass field after field; the deserted stands and dugouts are eerie in their silence. Like they're waiting for people to return, aching for the happy screams of little leaguers and parent-coaches.

And then I see Jay. He's on the last baseball field, standing by home plate, a baseball bat in one hand and a beer in the other. Empty bottles are strewn around his feet. I walk onto the field.

"Come on," I hear him shout. "Throw it."

Noah is at the pitcher's mound, winding up. But instead of throwing a real pitch, he tosses the ball underhand. It sails slowly toward Jay in a sad, wobbly arc. The only way it could be easier to hit is if it was an inflatable beach ball. Noah's no star athlete, but it's a lame throw even for him. Jay misses, not surprisingly. Like, *royally* misses. He swings the bat with his right hand and a little beer spills out of the beer bottle in his left. His feet cross, one over the other, he teeters and almost goes down. Kate runs over and steadies him.

"Aw, maaaan," Jay says, smiling. "So close! I can *taste* the homer, yo!"

I wonder how long they've been at this game. Throw Underhand to the Drunk. It's a new one—one I hope we won't have to play again any time soon.

"He hit it yet?" I ask.

"Nope," Kate says. She's still got her hands on Jay, holding him up.

"You're messing me up," Jay whines at her. "Let go."

"Fine, fall on your face," Kate mutters. She lets him go and he wobbles a bit but finds his balance. "Like you did three times in the last twenty minutes." She retreats and leans up against the blue dugout, then shoots me a weary glance. "You haven't missed much, believe me."

I can smell the beer on Jay's breath when I get within a five-foot radius of his "batting stance." Which right now involves a desperate lean to the left and a pitiful hunched-over posture.

"Dude," I say to him. "You're a mess."

"RIIIIILEY!" he says, beaming. "You're HERE! Awesome. We're playing *baseball*. We should try out for a *sports team*. It's AMAZING. Isn't it AMAZING?"

"Totally amazing," I say flatly. I notice how shiny-new his bat looks. "So that's what you were shopping for at Dick's? A bat and a baseball?"

"Hell yeah! And a mitt! Like my pops used to have. Just like my pops." He turns up his beer and drains it. "We used to play. And watch games on TV. It was *so cool*. Now I know why he always drank so much beer! Beer makes it SO FUN. Here," he drops the bat to his side and careens toward the case of Bud behind home plate. He pulls out a bottle and holds it out for me. "Have one, Riley. You'll be *amazed*."

I stare at him blankly and raise my eyebrows. "The cousin

with the fancy printer, right? That's how you got the case of beer. The fake ID."

"Are you a detective? I feel like I've asked you that before." Jay screws off the cap, apparently deciding to keep the beer for himself. Then he picks up the bat again. "You'd make a *great* detective."

Kate sits down in the grass and whips her hair into an elastic. "He's been like this since we got here. We tried to cut him off, but he got kind of nasty when we attempted to take his beer away. Wasn't pretty."

Noah comes in from the pitcher's mound. "You're just in time for a round of Entertain the Drunk," he says sadly. "Lucky you."

"Just please tell me he didn't cut that hole in the fence?" I say. "Tell me it was already there."

"Did you see his hand?" Noah asks.

I look at Jay's left hand, which other than having a death-grip on the bottle of beer, looks totally normal. But then I notice the right. It's a mess. He's got several cuts, a huge scab has formed over a few knuckles, and there are little streaks of blood on his shirtsleeve.

"So he also bought wire cutters," I say, sighing. I walk up to Jay and reach for the bat. "Can I see?"

He wobbles for a second and looks at me suspiciously. "You'll give it back?"

"Of course," I say.

"Okay. Here."

I gently take the bat and hand it to Noah. I hold Jay's hand in mine and look at the cut. It looks angry and painful, but it doesn't look like he needs stitches. Maybe just some Neosporin and Tylenol when the beer wears off.

I look behind Jay, toward the main pavilion in the complex.

I imagine a security guard emerging at any moment. I worry someone will spot the vandalized fence and call the cops. I'm surprised there isn't a guard watching the field in the first place. Plus, what the hell would we say if we were caught?

Well, Officer. My friend Jay here is pretty upset. His father just crossed to the other side, vanishing for all eternity right in front of Jay's eyes. His dad asked for forgiveness, but Jay completely screwed up and let his father leave this world without it. So, as you can see, he's had a rough day. Actually, we all have. How about you just give him a ticket and let us get on our way?

Kate joins me beside Jay. "I saw a spirit in and out of him for like the first twenty minutes we were here," she says, as if he weren't present. "Maybe we can just explain that to the cops, no problem. We'll just let them know that our beloved but damaged friend here let an evil spirit convince him to get super wasted and break into a ballpark. I'm sure the cop will understand."

"You saw a spirit?" Jay asks. "No way! Awesome! I missed another one. I'm *so bad* at hearing them. So amazingly bad!" Then he starts this horrible fake-laughing thing. And then it kind of changes into something else, something more like weeping. "Did you know my dad's gone?" he asks. He looks so pitiful all of a sudden. Almost like the little boy who found his dad dead at the bottom of the basement stairs. "Like, really gone?"

Noah walks over and gives Jay a hug. Another real one, not a bro hug. He squeezes his friend tightly and lets go. "We know, man," Noah says. "We know. It's going to be okay. Let's just get you home. You need a shower and about a gallon of water."

"You know what else?" Jay asks, pulling away from Noah. "I figured something out." He takes a long swig of beer. "Think about it. My dad could see spirits. Just like Peter. Just like we can. Because he wore the cross necklace, too. He had to deal with seeing this his whole life but didn't tell anybody. Couldn't. They wouldn't believe him. He needed to figure out that symbol, to figure it all out—" He stops and holds up the beer high in the air, like he's giving a toast. "No wonder he tried to drown it all out with booze. Can't blame him. But you know what? I did. I totally blamed him."

Jay looks at Noah, and then at me, and then at Kate. His brown eyes are rimmed with red and full of tears. I feel like I can still see the ten-year-old boy that he used to be. The one who watched baseball on TV with his dad, the one who rolled his eyes when his dad would try to talk about the cross necklace in the living room, why it was so valuable, why *nobody should ever touch it*. The one who wondered what was so magical about the liquid in his dad's martini glasses, why he always had to have one. Always.

"I'm sorry, man," Noah says, steadying Jay again. "But let's get you home. Okay?"

Jay looks up at the sky with goodbye written all over his face. Then he looks back at Noah.

"Okay," Jay says softly. "But bring the beer."

WE TAKE JAY TO his house and—no surprise—his mother isn't home. Kate gets the key from under the mushroom and opens the door. Jay has one arm around me and one arm around Noah, and together we guide him towards his bedroom.

"In the movies they always put people in the shower when they're wasted," Kate says. "With their clothes on. Always with their clothes on. Think that has merit?"

"Let's get naked!" Jay says. His breath nearly knocks me over. It's not only beer, but also something salty, something meaty, like . . . beef jerky. He must have had some leftover.

We pause at Jay's doorway.

"I say we bathe him fully clothed," Noah says to me over Jay's head as if Jay is not right here, hanging onto our necks like we're human crutches. Kate and I both nod.

The three of us manage to get Jay into the bathtub—clothes on—and he curls up in a ball and rests his head against the cold tub rim.

"Love," Jay says slowly. "*Love* this bathtub."

"Engage the water," Noah says. "I suggest cold."

"Engaging," Kate says as she cranks the shower on full blast. It sprays all over Jay—and us—and we expect him to sputter and spit and kind of snap out of his drunkenness.

Instead, he goes to sleep.

"Movies are just extended cultural lies," Kate says. "Why do they have to deceive us at every turn? From Disney princes to drunken showers. *Movies suck.*"

We let him get good and soaked and then turn the water off. It takes all three of us to pull a sopping, half-unconscious Jay out of the tub and into his bedroom. We're about to put him into his bed, wet clothes and all, but then I stop.

"Hold up," I mutter. "We can't put him in bed all wet like this. Like he's the uncool kid at a slumber party or something. That's just cruel."

"Oh, god," Noah says. "You want me to take off his pants. Okay. But I'm so going to hold this over his head *forever.*"

Noah holds Jay steady while Kate and I peel off his shirt, but then Noah goes to work on his jeans. It's not an easy job, pulling wet denim off a drunk person. But with effort Noah gets the job done.

"He can cope with sleeping in wet boxers," Noah says. "That's where I draw the line."

After tucking him in, we decide that it would *not* be a good idea to leave him alone in the house. I don't think he's drunk enough to have alcohol poisoning or anything, but you never know. Plus, we cannot let him try to get up and drunkenly fall down the stairs like his dad did. I can't even stand the thought.

"We keep watch," I say.

"I'm crashing on the nasty white sofa in the living room in front of the TV," Kate says. "And letting CMT lull me into relaxation."

"CMT?" Noah asks.

"Country music version of MTV," I say, smiling.

"I'll be outside then," Noah says.

"Dude, lay off the country music for once." It's Jay. He's suddenly roused from his slumber to half-mumble a defense of Kate's music choice. He smiles and then blinks his eyes slowly open and closed. "We gotta go easy. There are some good songs."

"Thanks, Jay," Kate says. "Even though you're drunk, I appreciate the backup. Now, rest. We'll all be outside if you need us."

"No. Riley," he says. "Here." He pats the bed next to him. "You two—outtie." He slurs his words a little and points toward the door.

Noah looks at me and raises his eyebrows. "Guess Jay wants a meeting with you," he says with a wistful smile. "Must have something important to say."

"OMG," Kate whispers. "Can we listen at the door?"

My heart pounds, but I roll my eyes. "Just go," I say. "I'll be out in a minute."

"We'll be right outside," Kate says. "With cups held up against the door so we can eavesdrop." She gives me a quick hug. "But wait. That works in the movies. Which probably means it *doesn't* work in real life." She sighs and heads out the door.

Noah raises his eyebrows at me again, and I give him the trust-me-I-have-no-idea-what's-going-on look in return. The door swooshes closed, leaving Jay and me shrouded in awkward silence. I go over and sit on the bed.

"Is there water?" Jay finally asks. I hand him the cup from his nightstand. "Awesome," he says and drains it. After a deep breath, he flops his head back down on the pillow. "I'm drunk."

"I'm aware," I say.

"I'm crap at this. You know that?"

I smile. "Sort of."

"These spirits. Can't hear them. Just can't." Jay groans. "What if I can't get over this? I mean, I messed up. Big."

I look up at the cracked plaster ceiling. "Well, you can give up. Be like an evil spirit—just mess with life. Or you can keep trying to get it right. Like the good spirits."

Jay manages a sleepy, crooked smile. But then I see something pass over his eyes, tiny ripples of worry. "You know I'm sorry, right?" he asks.

Then I realize it wasn't worry I saw; it was a spirit, a faint flicker.

"About?"

"That I couldn't like you back," he says, closing his eyes. "You know, like a girlfriend. I do love you, though. Always will. You know that, right?"

He knew. All this time.

But I don't feel a rush of embarrassment. I don't feel a

sudden need to don my armor of numbness. Instead, I feel something totally unexpected: relief. "I think we're both kind of bad at this," I tell him. "The whole figuring-out-what-to-do thing." I study his face; he looks so tired, so sad. "We'll get better at it though. We will."

He shoots me a look. It's kind, it's I'm sorry, it's—*still family?* He doesn't have to say anything else.

My eyes say it all:

Obviously. I love you, too.

Chapter 21

Sort of Beautiful

I leave Jay's room and find Kate asleep on the white couch in the living room with CMT blaring on the TV. Noah is out on the front porch. There are two beaten-up white wicker chairs, and he's in one of them. I head out the front door and sit on the other chair, and it creaks and groans under my weight.

"Cheap chairs," Noah says. "But I think they'll hold up."

"You sure?"

"Yes," he says. "Because there is a very recent *Horoscopes* magazine on the porch next to mine, which suggests someone has been doing some intense literary reading in this chair of late. So it must be sturdy."

I smile and lean back in my crappy chair and look up at the sky. The beautiful clear blue is fading; there's a storm cloud coming in from the west. The wind is picking up, and I see a few birds playing in the sky, riding the currents high up toward the clouds and then diving straight down over and over again.

"So did Jay, like, propose or something?" He sounds worn out. "Come to his senses?"

I keep my head back, my eyes focused on the birds looping in the sky. And go with the truth. "Jay's kind of messed up, isn't he?" I ask.

Noah doesn't answer right away. He sighs and leans back, too. "We all are. But he's a little more than most. Especially in the girl department," he adds, but not harshly. "And I knew you couldn't see it."

Before I can answer, the rain starts. *Hard.* It blows onto the porch and we jump up, stand against the house.

"Go in?" I ask.

"Please, no," he says. "I can hear the twang through the door. Don't make me go in there. Let's just . . . stay out here."

"In the rain?"

"We'll stay close to the house. We'll stay mostly dry."

So we do. But we don't stay dry. We sit down, side-by-side, getting sprayed by the rain that's blowing in.

"We're totally getting soaked," I say, even though I don't mind.

"Can I ask where you went earlier?" Noah asks.

"Because you've been the king of telling us where *you* go all the time . . ."

"True. And sorry."

"So *is* that where you were the whole time? At that professor's house in the cemetery?"

"Yeah," he says. He holds a hand out to catch a few raindrops. "I wanted his help, even before you guys wore the cross. But turns out he couldn't help all that much. They'd found the book but put it back thinking that might make it all stop. But it totally didn't." He looks at his rain-soaked shoes. "I'd hoped he could help me understand all the spirit stuff; I thought he might help me reach Cam. But now I just feel like I'll never get a chance."

I pull my knees up close to my chest. "I have something to tell you," I say. "That might help. My mom. She crossed. Through me."

"So she's—" Noah starts, but stops, unable to finish the question.

"Yeah," I say. "She's gone."

"You okay?"

I think about the joyride with Mom, how it felt to take that silver bird necklace and toss it off the bridge. How I felt this idea sing through my veins when her soul was in mine, that missing your own life in someone else's honor doesn't work. It doesn't honor anything or anyone; it just adds more sadness to the world. I think about how good it felt to drive with the windows down, my sunglasses on, the music up.

"I'm okay," I say. "And I think I figured something out: that even though someone might be sick, or sad, or gone, you have to live anyway. I think that's the best way to remember. So you don't forget them, but you don't let them stop you, either."

Noah's eyes soften as he looks into the storming sky. He nods.

"So I'm okay—in that way. Like, I'm hurt, but I'm okay at the same time. Make any sense?"

"Absolutely."

"And if you listen, maybe Cam will come to you, too. You'll get your chance."

Noah looks at me in a way he never has before, like he's happy and sad and wants to *say something* about it all. But he's afraid to.

I gently nudge him, asking.

"I was wrong," he finally says. "I thought I knew what I wanted to say to Cam. I thought I wanted to ask him why he did it. Why he left us." He pauses as the wind blows, his blond hair lifting in the breeze. "But I *know* why. He was in pain. And after the doctors couldn't fix him, and the meds couldn't fix him, and pot couldn't fix him, he just needed the pain to stop." His eyes fill with tears. That beautiful blue starts to glisten. Noah's eyes have always been the most beautiful among us; they've always been the most honest.

"You'll get a chance," I say softly. "I know it. Now that we understand this. You can be his doorway. Maybe he was just waiting for you to figure out what you needed to say."

Noah looks at me now, his sparkling eyes just barely more hopeful than sad. "I think I know what I need to tell him," he says. "I don't need to ask him why he did it, I need to tell him that I *know* why. And that I understand. I understand that when you're in pain, it's so much easier to make a bad choice. So much easier."

I feel tears well again. We sit for a minute, just listening to the storm, holding what we know between us.

"Those are some crazy dark clouds," he continues. "You can't even see an outline of the sun behind them. And don't bail on me when I say what I'm about to say." He leans into me, our shoulders touching. "But the clouds—they're like a coronagraph." I flash him a what-the-hell-is-a-coronagraph look. "Remember when I said I got one?" he asks. "When we were in Kate's basement?"

I shake my head. "Sorry. Not sure I was paying attention."

"Well," Noah says, running a hand through his damp hair, "a coronagraph is this thing that fits over a telescope when you're looking directly at the sun. It blocks out the direct light from the center so you can see stuff in the sun's atmosphere that would've been blotted out by the brightness. Like if you look at the sun without one, all you see is this blinding blob of light. But with a coronagraph, the main starlight is blocked out, and you can see the most amazing things in the sun's atmosphere that you would've missed—flares, coronal filaments, these crazy beautiful loops of light. It's amazing."

I don't say anything. I have no idea why we're talking about this.

"So," he continues, "I figured it out. That's how you have to see grief. Like it's a coronagraph, a lens to look at life through."

"I don't get it—" But I stop before I can finish my sentence because my stomach dives like those birds in the sky and my heart thunders in my chest right along with the storm.

Someone's here. A spirit.

"Like you," he says. He scoots a little closer, our legs touching, side-by-side now. He looks back up at the storming sky. "If I'd never been hurt, if I'd never been through anything, I might have only seen the bright stars like Sarah and those other super popular girls. And they'd blot out the *really* beautiful people. The people who sometimes get overshadowed—the intricate flares and filaments." He looks at me, *directly* at me, with those eyes. "I wouldn't wish what has happened to us on anyone. But if it hadn't happened, I would never have *seen* you—a beautiful, complicated loop of light."

It's the most beautiful thing anyone has ever said to me. And yet, it goes against what I thought earlier, what I said to my dad. It stands in the face of what I thought I'd learned.

"You don't think we're just damaged?" I ask softly. "That all we have in common is what we lost? All the grief? That we're just some messed-up club?"

"Not at all," he says. He gently tucks a wet strand of my brown hair behind my ear. "I don't think what we share is grief, I think we share what grief has let us see."

I close my eyes and flash warm all over despite the chill

of the rain. I feel so . . . seen. Like he said. Like I've been building a bonfire and waving flags and jumping up and down trying to get Jay's attention for years, but Noah has quietly spotted me all along. Like he's taken this loss we all share and turned it on its head, made something beautiful, waded through it, eyes wide open.

I open my eyes again and expect to see Noah's eyes still looking back at me, but I don't. I see a flash of someone else's.

"Spirits," I whisper.

Noah smiles. "Oh yeah? And what do you think they want?"

"I think they're trying to get us to . . ." I pause. I take a breath; I get quiet. I feel chills up and down my arms, my heart pounding as fast as hummingbird wings.

The way to help the dead is by living.

And I kiss him. Like *really* kiss him. I've never kissed a boy before, not like this. And I *feel* it. From the top of my head, past my glued-together heart, all the way down to my unpainted toenails. I'm two places at once—forever in this moment, on this porch, grounded by this kiss, this warmth, this now-ness, and simultaneously soaring in the storming sky. Swooping like dizzy birds, unafraid of rushing dark clouds. And then I soar twenty feet higher, let the ground get smaller and smaller— because he's kissing back. And kissing back and kissing back. And it's so alive. Here. Now. The next right thing.

And then I notice it, a feeling like a rush of warm wind. A tear makes its way down my cheek. I gently pull away from Noah's lips, and the spirits are gone. It's just us now.

"They're gone," I say, smiling. "Crossed. Through us."

"That's—" he stops, searching for the perfect words.

"Sort of beautiful?"

"Absolutely," he says, kissing me again. Lightly. Like a brush of spirit. "Absolutely."

History Behind Signs of You

Although *Signs of You* is a work of fiction, the Jesuit concept of the "discernment of spirits" is not.

The biography of Ignatius of Loyola—the one that Jay reads to Riley and to Kate—is an accurate sketch of Ignatius's early life. It is true that in 1522 he scribbled down revelations he had during a mystical experience by the Cardoner River in Spain. They would later evolve into what is widely considered one of the world's theological masterpieces, *The Spiritual Exercises*.

The insights that Ignatius inscribed in those pages continue to enjoy broad appeal. Although a small part of a larger Ignatian philosophy, the discernment of spirits is still taught today. Nearly five hundred years ago, Ignatius provided this putative tool to alert us when spirits enter and influence us. Moreover, he believed that if we get quiet and pay attention to their movements, we can discern what the spirits are trying to get us to do. People of all faiths are taken through the *Exercises* at retreat centers around the world.

When I stumbled upon this idea, it completely captured

my imagination. I read everything that I possibly could about the subject, and then added fictional twists and turns.

The result is this novel.

The first draft of the *Exercises,* handwritten by Ignatius, has not survived. In my novel, the characters discover the original manuscript he wrote after his mystical experience. While it is unlikely that it would be discovered in a tidy book format or that its contents are much different from the versions that were later published, it is true that Ignatius *did* write down his initial insights and they *are* missing. So I asked myself what might be hidden in his original notes. I let myself imagine what it would be like to see his ideas come to life, to see spirits at work influencing the choices of the living. I researched the languages Ignatius would have used to express his theories and the idea that he would make notes in a mix of Basque, Spanish, and made-up Latin has historical merit.

The premise of *Signs of You* is based on the concept of spirit discernment found in the *Exercises,* and my characters use some of Ignatius's actual spirit tests. Yet my novel employs the term "spirits" in a way that Ignatius and modern Jesuits do not. When Ignatius wrote of spirits, he wasn't referring to the individual souls of the deceased as Riley discovers in the book, but to broader notions of the Holy Trinity, which complied with his own 16th century Catholic teachings. Part of the real-life historical controversy surrounding Ignatius concerned his ideas about finding spiritual guidance in everyday experiences. In short, he was ahead of his time.

The Lost Cross is also a figment of my imagination. As far as I know, St. Ignatius was not wearing a necklace when he had his revelation by the Cardoner River. I needed a tangible object, a relic, to connect my characters to the saint, and the cross necklace served that purpose well.

However, the word that is inscribed on the back of the cross—*magis*—is a term frequently used by Ignatius and by modern Jesuits. Its Latin meaning is *more*, and Ignatius used it to ask himself what more he could do or strive to be. I gave it a hidden meaning—that there was more to his spirit discernment theory that was never published. As part of my research I visited a Jesuit university campus and saw the word *magis* inscribed on buildings and walkways.

Finally, while Ignatius's squiggly line puzzle in *Signs of You* is fiction, the Jesuit seal and Latin phrases my characters use to crack it are very real. The Jesuit seal does bear the initials I.H.S., an abbreviation of Jesus's name in Greek. If the nails below stood for a "V," the seal would read I.H.S.V., or *in hoc signo vinces*, Latin for "in this sign, conquer." However, as far as I know, the only letters meant to appear on the seal are I.H.S.

Emily France
September 2015

P.S. If you are curious about my research, here are some of my favorite sources:

Ganss, George E. *The Spiritual Exercises of St. Ignatius: A Translation and Commentary*. Chicago: Loyola Press, 1992.

Text of the *Exercises* with commentary. This is not the best place to begin research, but the rules for the discernment of spirits can be found in the last section.

Kapell, Jason. "The Olive." Online video clip. YouTube, 4 Feb. 2009. Web. 4 Sept. 2015.

An entertaining video profile of Ignatius.

Lacouture, Jean. *Jesuits: A Multibiography*. Trans. Jeremy Leggatt. Washington, D.C.: Counterpoint, 1995.
A biography covering five hundred years of history and Jesuit influence.

Martin, James. *The Jesuit Guide to Almost Everything: A Spirituality for Real Life*. New York: HarperCollins, 2010.
An excellent place to begin research on the subject, this is an accessible source that gives an overview of Ignatian philosophy and of discernment.

O'Malley, John W. *The First Jesuits*. Cambridge, MA: Harvard University Press, 1993.
An often cited, classic work on the first members of the society.

O'Malley, John W. *The Jesuits: A History from Ignatius to the Present*. London: Rowman & Littlefield, 2014.
A concise summary of Jesuit history through Pope Francis. It contains a thorough list of titles for further reading, including sources that are critical of the society.

Acknowledgments

Working with Dan Ehrenhaft is like being in the Exhilarating Collaboration Montage of a movie titled *The Editor*. His mix of genius, kindness, and belief in my work is the stuff of a writer's dreams. I hit the lottery when Soho said yes; thank you for making me a better writer.

To the entire team at Soho Teen, thank you for publishing my debut novel. I hope you know what a difference you have made in my life.

Having Jennifer Unter as my agent is like having my own personal cavalry. Complete with bugles and flags. Thank you for championing my work and for making my greatest dream become a reality. I am so grateful for you.

I owe many thanks to those who helped me with research. It was nothing short of a joy. Thanks to Professor Carole Newlands at the University of Colorado Classics Department (CU Boulder) for her help with Latin. To Alison Hicks, the Spanish, Portuguese, and Catalan Librarian at CU Boulder for her help locating Basque translations of the *Exercises*. To Josh Hadro, Deputy Director of the New York Public Library

Labs. To the Sacred Heart Jesuit retreat center and Father E. Edward Kinerk, S.J. for taking me through an abbreviated version of the *Exercises*. Staying in my spare room there and eating our silent meals was a grand adventure.

I must acknowledge those who have given me the courage to dream big. Thanks to my professors at Brown University and especially to Professor Howard Chudacoff, who encouraged me as a history student. Your classes will forever sparkle in my mind. Thanks to my law professors JoEllen Lind, Rosalie Levinson, and Robert Blomquist. Acing a Blomquist Grilling about Latin phrases in a case (while I quaked with fear) is one of my greatest memories. Thanks to the *Valparaiso Law Review* for making me the Editor in Chief. I still draw confidence from that appointment. And I'm sorry for the *Blue Book* errors I missed; I was secretly stealing time to work on this novel. Mea culpa.

Thanks to my MFA writing instructors Michael White, Elizabeth Searle, Suzanne Strempek Shea, Lewis Robinson, and Dennis Lehane. And to my critique partner of over a decade, Tara Thomas, for battling the crickets year after year. Thanks also to my high school creative writing teacher, Kathy Jacobs, who told me I could.

To my dear friends who have stuck with me, thank you: Kristen Fout, Jennifer Smith, Megan Smith, Lauren Fox, and my entire Boulder crew. Thanks to all the Colorado writers in my life for your support.

A writer could not ask to have better parents than the erudite, colorful, lovers-of-the-arts, Stuart and Ann Calwell. They are two of the most deeply good and honorable human beings I have ever known. Thank you for letting me fly and for cheering my unconventional path in the skies. I love you.

Love to Elisa Rushworth, the greatest sister in all of

recorded history. You are a treasure to me. Love to the rest of my fantastic family: Rushy, Abigail, Harry, Brittney, Patrick. And to the world's most loving in-laws, Kevin and Sue France. I adore all of you.

And to my beloved astronomer husband, Kevin, who has known me since I was the junior high Queen of the Nerd Herd: Thank you for loving me like you do and for believing in this book from the first word. You are the most magnificent person I have ever known, reader of every page, partner in every step. Oh, how I love you.